"What a smashing vacation this is turning out to be," said Gwen.

I've flown through the universe, thought Sabrina, *hitched a ride on a shooting star and kissed Harvey Kinkel.* But swimming underwater near the reefs—actually feeling the touch of a school of fish darting past—definitely an all-time high. Sabrina walked a few steps ahead of Gwen, and knelt down to inspect a bright blue shell.

When she looked up, something flickered in the water farther down the beach. The light was so intense, she had to shield her eyes from the reflection. "What's that?" she asked Gwen.

"Oh, no!" Gwen cried. "I think it's a dolphin."

They ran down the beach, stunned to see a large tail covered in shiny scales moving in the shallow water. When they were a few yards away, they stopped dead in their tracks. The sparkling fish tail was the bottom half of a gorgeous guy!

"Gwen, it's not a dolphin . . ."

A merman?

Sabrina, the Teenage Witch® books

Available from ARCHWAY Paperbacks

Sabrina
The Teenage Witch®

Sabrina Down Under

A Novelization by Ellen Titlebaum
Based on the television movie
written by Daniel Berendsen

Based on Characters Appearing in Archie Comics

And based upon the television series
Sabrina, The Teenage Witch
Created for television by Nell Scovell
Developed for television by Jonathan Schmock

AN ARCHWAY PAPERBACK
Published by POCKET BOOKS
New York   London   Toronto   Sydney   Singapore

AN ARCHWAY PAPERBACK *Original*

An Archway Paperback published by
POCKET BOOKS, a division of Simon & Schuster Inc.
1230 Avenue of the Americas, New York, NY 10020

ISBN: 0-671-04752-3

First Archway Paperback printing November 1999

10 9 8

AN ARCHW
registered tr

SABRINA
logos and c   ;, Inc.

Printed in the

IL5+

For Libby, the good witch of the East;
her magic teaches, enlightens and inspires

Sabrina Down Under

Chapter 1

Sabrina sat close to the large window of the helicopter, gazing at the open ocean below. *I can't believe I'm finally on vacation,* she thought. *Far away from homework and curfews, witch training tests and getting up early... Sabrina smiled at the thought of Harvey and playfully twirled her blond hair. And yes, far away from Harvey... but I'm only away for a week, and whenever I close my eyes I see his handsome face smiling down at me ... Besides, now's my chance to see my best witch friend, Gwen!*

Suddenly, schools of brightly colored fish caught her eye as they disappeared momentarily inside a huge coral formation. *This is more beautiful than anything I could conjure up,* she thought with a smile.

"There it is!" cried Sabrina. "The Great Barrier Reef."

The pilot smiled, his handsome face weathered from the sun. "That's a piece of her, anyway. She goes on for another two thousand kilometers."

Wow, thought Sabrina. *Will Gwen and I have time to explore all of that?* Sabrina laughed, remembering how much fun she and Gwen had had in Rome. They had solved a four-hundred-year-old mystery, met some super hunky guys, and enjoyed some of the most amazing art in the world. At least, *she* had been blown away by the art. Gwen had just managed to turn Bernini's statue of David into a real, live guy with a thing for jellybeans and slingshots . . .

Half-submerged coral reefs were laid out across the turquoise sea like a never-ending necklace. It sparkled gold, brown and orange against the blue-green sea. "It's even more beautiful than I'd imagined," said Sabrina softly.

"First time down under?" asked the pilot.

"Yeah." Sabrina nodded. "Though for being 'down under' everything is surprisingly right side up! I've wanted to come ever since I read this fantastic book about the reef," she said, pulling a book out of her bag. "Here it is. *The Secrets of the Reef* by Dr. Julian Martin."

The pilot chuckled. "Now there's a bloke who spends more time underwater than most fish."

"Fortunately for us, he writes better than most of

them, too. His research institute is attached to the resort. Supposedly, guests can dive with—look!" Sabrina pointed to a group of dolphins leaping playfully in the clear sea. "We crash, I die happy. It's hard to imagine there's a whole other universe just below the surface," said Sabrina, unable to look away from the window. Suddenly, her eyes narrowed. Something was down there that looked more like a man than a dolphin.

"Did you see that?" she asked incredulously.

"What? Something in the water?"

"Yeah. Hurry, turn around. I think I saw someone," said Sabrina, peering below.

The pilot quickly turned the helicopter back and hovered low over the water. "Are you sure you saw someone? We're too far out, even for divers."

After a long look, Sabrina turned back to the pilot. "It was just a flash, but I could have sworn . . . Sorry, I guess twenty-two hours on a plane is catching up with me."

"Not a problem," said the pilot, turning the helicopter toward land. "The reef is always playin' tricks on people."

Sabrina watched the shadow of the helicopter dart across the liquid blue of the sea. *I know I saw someone out there,* she thought. *I just know it . . .*

Long after the helicopter had disappeared from the sky, the dark outline of a man appeared on the coral. He pulled himself onto the reef, his long fish tail fluttering in the waves. Then he gracefully slipped back into the water, the sun shimmering off the scales on his tail. With a sudden, blinding flash, he vanished into the clear sea.

The helicopter began its descent onto Hamilton Island. The island was green and lush, surrounded by milky-white beaches and crystal clear water. From her aerial view, Sabrina could see boats swaying in the water by the marina, palm trees blowing in the sandy air by the beach, and past the resort she could make out the beginning of the wildlife sanctuary. Forests of thick tropical trees spread out for miles, untouched by developers. She could almost see the wallabies hopping, and hear the bright green parrots singing for her arrival. Sabrina was so excited to be here and to see her best witch friend, Gwen, that she could hardly keep still.

"There it is. Hamilton Island. Home to some of the best diving in the world," said the pilot, as the helicopter touched the landing pad.

"Yes!" cried Sabrina happily. Gwen was standing nearby, waving frantically. She looked really good. She was wearing a red tank top that made her short, chestnut-brown hair shine, and a long, black wrap-around skirt. Her clear plastic bag, stuffed with jellybeans, a camera, suntan lotion and this month's edition of *Young Witch* magazine, glittered in the morning sun. Sabrina laughed at the jellybeans, remembering Gwen's long-standing passion for anything sweet.

A porter opened the helicopter door and helped Sabrina out. He gently placed a shell necklace around her neck and said, "G'day. Welcome to Hamilton Island."

Delighted with her necklace, Sabrina smiled warmly and said, "G'day to you, too."

"Sabrina!" shrieked Gwen, running up to her and giving her a big hug. *I forgot how cool Gwen's English accent sounds,* Sabrina thought, hugging her friend tightly.

"Gwen! It's so good to see you. You look great! How long have you been here?" But before Gwen could answer, two fishermen passed by arguing loudly. They were carrying pails and fishing rods, but curiously, no fish.

". . . I'm telling you, two hours ago my bait turned into a kangaroo and hopped away," one of the fishermen said angrily.

Sabrina rolled her eyes and turned to Gwen. "I've been here about two hours," said Gwen, looking away.

"Gwen, you promised me that you wouldn't use your magic on this vacation." Sabrina sighed. *When you had magic, it was hard not to conjure and point whenever you felt like it. But magic has consequences, and I don't want to deal with all that here. I'm on vacation! Just a regular sheila enjoying the sun and sea . . .*

5

"But I've been practicing. I'm really a lot better than the last time you saw me. Watch," said Gwen, clenching her fist. The shells on Sabrina's necklace magically grew into tropical flowers.

"Wicked! Told you I've been practicing," said Gwen happily.

"Yeah, and it would have been perfect . . . if you hadn't just given me a tail!" Sabrina turned around to show off her brand-new bunny tail. A porter, his arms full of luggage, nearly fell over at the sight of Sabrina's fluffy, white tail.

"In my defense," said Gwen, pouting, "I didn't say I was good, I just said I was better."

Sabrina grinned and with a quick point of her finger she was tailless once more.

Soon, Sabrina and Gwen were walking past one of the resort's pools. The place was hopping! People were lounging on deck chairs, relaxing at the pool bar, and splashing in the clear blue water.

"Coming here is the best idea you ever had, Sabrina. This place has absolutely everything," said Gwen with a smile. Her smile grew even bigger as a very cute guy walked by, carrying a surfboard. "And I mean everything," she added.

"I know two things it doesn't have," said Sabrina. "Salem and Stoney. I can't believe we've finally managed to escape our furry chaperones."

Sabrina's cat, Salem, was her familiar. He was really a warlock who was forced to spend time as a cat for trying to take over the human world. Now, he spent most of his time eating too much, napping, and generally being a major pain in her life. Gwen's familiar was a fluffy hamster named Stonehenge, who delighted in making fun of Gwen's conjuring skills.

"Do you think a week is long enough to rebuild my self-esteem?" asked Gwen. They looked at each other and laughed happily. *Free at last!*

As Sabrina and Gwen made their way to their room, two porters passed by carrying luggage and a cat case. They opened the door to a luxurious suite and placed the cat case on a dresser.

"You ever seen this Saberhagen guy?" one of the porters asked as he opened the blinds, revealing a stunning view of the beach.

"Nah. No one has. And he's been coming here for years," replied the other porter, sticking his finger into the cat case to pet the black feline inside. "What kinda nut spends a week locked in a hotel room with a mangy cat—ow! This thing bit me! I'll probably need to get a shot," he added as they left the room.

"And I'll need to wash my mouth out. *Ptui!*" snarled Salem from his cramped quarters. The cat case popped open, and Salem sauntered out. "Note to self. Get a case with more leg room. And better movies." Salem leapt onto the table and caught a glimpse of the breathtaking view. *For someone who almost ruled the world, this is more like it.* "Hello, paradise!"

"Hello, paradise," said Sabrina, walking into their tropical bungalow. The room was airy and comfortable and smelled like an ocean breeze. The sun spilled in through two large glass doors that faced the water. The twin beds were separated by a small table and were covered in sea-blue bedspreads. Sabrina threw her bag onto the bed and emptied the contents. Leftover apples from the plane, bottled water, and a camera lay scattered on the bed. *I can't wait to take pictures and show Harvey—he would love this place,* she thought with a grin. Sabrina ran to the bathroom and slipped on her favorite flowered bikini and grabbed a beach towel. She made a quick call to her aunts back in New England so they'd know she'd arrived, and then she took Gwen's hand, and they skipped outside onto their private deck. "So, what are we waiting for? Let's get this vacation started," said Sabrina.

Giggling, Sabrina and Gwen raced down the steps of their bungalow and ran toward the resort's open-air lobby. The room was bursting with activity. People were shopping in the gift shop and eating in the snack bar nearby. Others were lounging on the sofas, gazing at the waves breaking onto the shore and the sunbathers lounging in deck chairs by the pool. Potted palm trees lined the walls, and vases full of tropical flowers scented the room. A

table was piled high with refreshments and brochures about diving in the coral reefs and hiking in
the wildlife sanctuary. Gwen eagerly picked up
one of the brochures and began reading aloud. "We
can go windsurfing, snorkeling, hiking, water-ski-
ing . . ."

"First thing we have to do is find a dive shop," interrupted Sabrina. Out of the corner of her eye,
Gwen noticed a guy with an amazing smile heading
toward the beach with snorkeling equipment. "Did I
mention they have snorkeling?" asked Gwen with a
mischievous grin. Sabrina laughed and pulled Gwen
past the front desk and toward the dive shop.

Hilda Spellman whirled around the living room,
her silver sequined gown twinkling in the soft glow
of candlelight.

"Hmm . . . something's missing," she said with a
slight frown. Then, she pointed and the living room
was transformed into a fairy-tale ballroom. Dozens
of men in black tuxedos danced with beautiful
ladies in long, white gowns. A string quartet played
in the corner, and everywhere, drops of glitter,
sparkles and magic dust swirled in the perfumed air.

"Dum dee dum ta dee," she sang gaily, twirling
and spinning to the music. Suddenly, a dashing man
entered the ballroom. He was twice as tall and twice
as good-looking as every other man there.

The music stopped. The dancers stopped in mid-
twirl and stared. A hush filled the room. He crossed

the floor in several strides and knelt at Hilda's feet, a single white rose in his hand. She caressed the petals and gazed deeply into his dark, mysterious eyes . . .

"Not the mysterious stranger in the ballroom fantasy again," snapped Zelda, pushing past the imaginary quartet. Her blond hair was pulled back, and she had on what Sabrina called her New England librarian attire; a long skirt, matching sweater set, and practical shoes. Her favorite new book, *Physics for Witches,* was tucked under one arm.

"Now that Sabrina's away for a week, I was thinking we should do something *useful* with our free time," she continued in her older sister voice. "It's such a nice feeling to be *purposeful,* Hilda."

Hilda sighed, and with a quick, regrettable point, the dancers, quartet and ballroom disappeared in a swirl of sparkles. She pointed herself into a leather miniskirt and a tiger-spotted silk shirt.

"You know, Zelda, we should use this time to relax. To enjoy our powers freely," said Hilda, plopping down onto the couch.

The two sisters had given up their glamorous life of intergalactic jet-setting witches when they assumed the guardianship of their brother's daughter, Sabrina. Zelda felt it was important that they showed Sabrina a stable home life, even if they *were* witches. So, they had both agreed to cut out the fancy living.

"Well, can't we enjoy our powers and do something worthwhile?" Zelda countered.

"As long as my man of mystery can come along, and you leave me out of whatever science projects you have in mind, that's fine with me," said Hilda, smiling broadly.

"It was so nice of Sabrina to call us. I do hope she gets a chance to see some of the exotic undersea life while she's there," said Zelda.

Hilda sat up eagerly. "Oh yes! I hope she sees kangaroos and rides on a dolphin and meets some good-looking guys . . ."

Zelda laughed. She couldn't help but feel a little excited herself—their Sabrina was on an adventure!

Hilda jumped off the couch and faced her sister with a look of mischievous delight. "I've got a great idea!" she cried. "It's not terribly *purposeful,* but I'm sure you could think of a way to *make* it purposeful—let's surprise Sabrina! Let's go to Australia!"

"Well . . ." said Zelda, crossing her arms on her chest. "There is a lot to learn about marine life in the Great Barrier Reef . . . not to mention cleaning up toxic waste dumps. And there's always the problem of overfishing . . . okay! Let's do it!"

The two sisters giggled with anticipation. Hilda closed her eyes, concentrated and pointed. The Spellman sisters were on their way . . .

The phone rang loudly at the front desk, and the manager, David Hadley, answered. "Mr. Saberhagen! I didn't realize you'd arrived," he said nervously. He covered the mouthpiece with his hand and barked angrily at his staff, "Why didn't anyone tell me Mr. Saberhagen had arrived?"

Back in his palatial suite, Salem was talking to the manager on speakerphone. He had already picked through the tropical fruit in the welcome basket and had successfully finished two jars of macadamia nuts.

"Nice fruit basket. Though you cheaped out on the macadamia nuts," drawled Salem, clicking his nails against the deep mahogany desk.

"I'll send some up immediately. I need nuts," he mouthed to his staff.

"You remember the drill, don't you?" asked Salem.

"Of course. No one is ever to enter your room unannounced. And your cat Salem has complete and total access to the resort. The staff has already been alerted." David covered the mouthpiece again and cried, "Alert the staff!" He wiped his brow and turned his full attention back to Mr. Saberhagen. "Your cat's every whim is our desire."

Salem laid out his newest copy of *Catmopolitan* and said almost pleasantly, "Like it. Remind me to needlepoint that on a pillow. Now, patch me through to room service, pronto."

Later that afternoon, Sabrina emerged from the ocean carrying a mask and snorkel. She plopped onto a chair in the shallow water and dangled her legs in the gentle waves. She looked up and smiled—Gwen was walking toward her with that cute guy from the lobby. *Oh boy,* thought Sabrina, *Gwen and her crushes—she sure doesn't waste any time. How long has she been here, four hours? He sure is cute though. . . .*

"Sabrina, this is Jerome. Jerome, Sabrina," said Gwen, beaming from head to toe.

"Pleasure, Sabrina," said Jerome in a very thick Australian accent. "Just tellin' your pommy cobber here that I was afraid there may be too many Steak 'n' Kidneys about, but not the case, eh? I'll pop and get us some lolly water. Hooroo." After that amazing speech, he headed off to the little beach bar.

Gwen sighed loudly. "Doesn't he have the cutest accent?"

"Can't understand a word he says, can you?" asked Sabrina, stifling a laugh.

Gwen grinned. "No. I was hoping you could."

"Sorry," said Sabrina. "But who cares . . . He's got dimples the size of coconuts."

While Jerome picked up three soft drinks, a black cat sat farther down the bar sipping a huge fruity drink stuffed with colored umbrellas.

"Ah," said Salem, taking a sip. "Fruity, tropical . . . and cold. Ow, ow, brain freeze." But a little headache wasn't about to come between Salem and his refreshment. He finished his drink in one long, loud, and icy gulp.

Jerome greeted the girls with a grin as he handed out the soft drinks. "You know, I could go for a bite. What say you to some sammies or dog eyes?"

Sabrina and Gwen exchanged a meaningful look.

"A little slower and in English?" suggested Sabrina.

"Preferably, the Queen's," added Gwen good-naturedly.

Suddenly, loud voices shouted angrily from down the beach. Two divers were yelling at a man who was trying to take their dive bag.

"Let go of me! You can't open that!" cried one of the divers.

The dive bag spilled open, revealing bits of coral and marine life. "A couple of bloody poachers are what you two are," said the man. The two divers took off down the beach.

"How'd you like it if somebody swam into your home and broke off your arms?" The man called after them. "Well, you'll know how it feels if I ever catch you on my reef again."

"That's him!" cried Sabrina. "That's Dr. Martin."

"The marine biologist?" asked Jerome. "He sounds as mad as a gumtree full of galahs."

"He's not crazy, he's brilliant," explained Sabrina. "He's the one who wrote the book I sent you, remember, Gwen? Didn't you just love—You never read it, did you?"

"I meant to. Really," said Gwen, blushing. "But I've been busy—you try and find a decent bathing suit in London . . ."

Sabrina walked down the beach to Dr. Martin. He was kneeling on the wet sand, sorting through the stolen marine life and coral. Sabrina took a deep breath, cleared her throat and said, "Dr. Martin, hi, I'm Sabrina. I'm a huge fan of yours. I've read practically everything you've written. I'm actually thinking about becoming—"

"Look at this!" exclaimed Dr. Martin. He pulled out a tropical fish stashed in a jar. "They were going to sell it. Probably to some idiot who wants it just because it matches their drapes." He knelt at the water's edge and set the beautiful fish free.

Sabrina, with a lot less confidence, continued, "—becoming a marine biologist and was wondering if . . ."

Dr. Martin picked up a piece of pilfered coral. "Dead," he muttered. "Broke it right off. Do you have any idea how long this took to grow?" he demanded.

"I think that's *Scleractiria,* one of the slowest growing corals. So, about three hundred years?" she said timidly.

A smile slowly formed on Dr. Martin's face. "That's right. What did you say your name was?"

He seemed genuinely interested.

"Sabrina."

Dr. Martin stood up. "Julian Martin," he said kindly. "I get a little worked up when people mess with my reef. Marine biologist, eh?"

"Thinking about it."

"Hopefully my tirade hasn't dissuaded you. You know, I'm leading a dive tomorrow morning and I'd be honored if—"

"First name on the list!" cried Sabrina happily.

Chapter 2

The sun slowly rose over Hamilton Island, casting a gentle glow over the waves and the old wooden dock in the harbor. Sabrina was in her wet suit, hurrying down the dock with her flippers tucked under her arm.

"Hurry up," she called to Gwen, who was lagging behind. Gwen yawned loudly and replied, "Why? The fish aren't even awake yet."

Jerome, however, was wide awake, and jogged eagerly down the dock. "Mornin', Gwen," he said sheepishly. Gwen's eyes popped open and she smiled warmly. "Jerome! Nothing like an exhilarating dive to start your day. Practically had to toss my roommate out of bed."

Sabrina rolled her eyes and waved at Dr. Martin,

who was waiting for them in his inflatable Zodiac at the end of the dock.

Soon, they were sitting on the edge of the Zodiac with Dr. Martin and his divers, speeding across the ocean toward the coral reefs.

Back at the resort, Salem was relaxing on a lounge chair by the pool. A waiter adjusted his chair to its full reclining position, and fluffed up the pillows behind his furry black head. "Your pineapple punch . . . sir," said a waiter. Salem sighed contentedly, and took a satisfying gulp. Just then, a second waiter appeared and said, "When you're done here that crazy lady's Persian could use another shrimp cocktail." The first waiter shrugged. "That's what I get for being a cat person."

Salem immediately perked up and looked down the long row of lounge chairs. Sure enough, past two teenage girls, the family from Sydney and the elderly widow, sat the most beautiful cat Salem had ever seen. Salem watched her delicately pick up a shrimp, dip it into some sauce and then gently place it into her perfectly whiskered mouth. After carefully licking her paws, the Persian stretched her four shapely legs, and shook out her stunning fur.

"Well, hello pretty lady," said Salem. "If she's really a cat, then I'm a monkey's uncle. Oh, wait, I forgot, my sister married an orangutan . . ."

* * *

Dr. Martin stopped the Zodiac over the dive sight. As everyone began adjusting their gear, he said, "There's a lot more to this experience than just pretty colors. There is life everywhere you look. We are guests here. It's important to remember that. All right then. Tanks checked? Everyone got a buddy?"

Jerome turned to Gwen. "Gwen, what do you say? You and me?"

Gwen blushed. She felt warm and happy all over. "I'd love to—"

"Gwen!" interrupted Sabrina.

". . . if I hadn't already promised . . . ah . . . ," Gwen mumbled.

Sabrina rolled her eyes. "Sabrina."

"Right," said Gwen. "Sabrina."

They checked each other's tanks and put on their mouthpieces and masks. *This is going to be so cool,* thought Sabrina, her heart pounding inside her wet suit.

SWOOSH! SWOOSH!

Sabrina and Gwen rolled backward off the Zodiac and into the turquoise sea. The reef wall surrounded them, sloping steeply to the ocean floor. The reef was a myriad of oranges, browns and yellows. The strange, twisted formations seemed oddly graceful underwater. They followed a school of brightly colored fish through an opening in the coral and found themselves in a magical underworld paradise. Clown fish puffed up their cheeks and darted around the sea anemones on the sandy bottom. Sabrina and

Gwen held hands as a black sea snake slithered past them, on his way up to the surface for air. They swam near some lush green plants and tried not to rub against the rough coral when a school of bright blue surgeonfish scattered past.

Sabrina was so thrilled she wanted to get Gwen's attention, but it was impossible to make herself understood with the dive gear on. She had promised herself she wouldn't use magic unless it was absolutely necessary. But this was *definitely* a had-to moment. She let some air out of her mouthpiece, flicked her hand across the bubble, and watched it magically grow. It grew into a shimmering, translucent circle of air, and Sabrina and Gwen quickly popped their heads inside and took out their mouthpieces.

"Wicked," said Gwen.

"Isn't this the most incredible experience you've ever had? Don't you wish we could stay down here forever?" gushed Sabrina.

"You mean after Jerome teaches me to windsurf, right?" joked Gwen.

"Wait a minute," said Sabrina, "I don't need to wish." She put her mouthpiece back on.

"Sabrina, please don't do anything—"

Pop! Gwen was suddenly surrounded by millions of tiny bubbles. She pushed through them just in time to watch Sabrina transform herself into a beautiful, multicolored fish! *Whoo-hoo!*

"Scales. Very in this year," said Sabrina. Gwen

gave her a big thumbs-up. Sabrina waved a silky fin and darted through an opening in the coral.

Back at the pool, the lovely Persian sporting the dark sunglasses happily sunned herself. She casually turned the pages of *Vanity Fair*, comforted that her half-finished shrimp cocktail and fruit smoothie remained in easy reach on the little table next to her. Her reverie was disturbed by the sudden appearance of Salem at the foot of her chaise longue.

"Hello. My name is Saberhagen, Salem Saberhagen. I couldn't help noticing that we have a lot in common." Salem strutted close to her face and flicked her sunglasses with his tail. "We wear the same brand of sunglasses and we're both people trapped in the body of a cat."

The Persian let out a deep sigh, and said in a sexy purr, "I'm Hillary. And at the risk of starting a conversation, what gave me away?"

"I don't know, maybe a certain something in your eyes. Or that copy of *Vanity Fair* you're reading. So, what do you say, Hillary? You, me, the moon, some catnip?"

Hillary leaned closer to Salem, and said flirtatiously, "You know what I say, Salem . . ."

"Yes?" he asked breathlessly.

"I say, I didn't fall for creeps like you when I was a woman, so I'm certainly not going to fall for them now that I'm a cat." Hillary gave him one last withering look and leapt away.

"I'll take that as a maybe. Ooh, shrimp," said Salem, helping himself to the rest of her shrimp cocktail.

Sabrina swam through the coral, investigating the endless holes and caves at the reef's edge. "Only one drawback to being a fish," she said. "Saltwater. Bleck!" Just then, a beautiful fish swam so close to her, she could feel the softness of its fins. "The blue-spot butterfly fish. Hey," Sabrina called. "Don't you know you're supposed to be extinct?" The little fish swam into an opening in the rock and disappeared.

"Fish. Cute, but lousy conversationalists."

Gwen burst up to the surface and took off her mouthpiece and her mask. "Sabrina's so good," she said aloud. "With my luck, I'd have turned myself into the Loch Ness Monster."

Suddenly, Gwen felt a hand on her shoulder and heard a man say, "Excuse me." She screamed and turned around, and found herself face to face with a gorgeous guy not wearing any diving gear. He screamed as well.

"What a funny way to say hello. Where I come from we usually just shake hands," said the man.

"Sorry," said Gwen. "You startled me."

"Well," he continued, "I'm startled to meet you, too."

* * *

Sabrina saw the blue-spot butterfly fish again and darted after it. The little fish disappeared into a small crevice in the coral. "Little fish, come back," said Sabrina, peering into the hole. But instead of the blue-spot butterfly fish, a moray eel shot out of the tiny opening! Sabrina dived out of its way and landed smack into a school of angelfish. The angelfish had flat, disklike bodies that carried long fins and beautifully splayed tails. Some were silver, some marbled with different colors, some had a reddish hue, and all of them were bumping and grinding directly into Sabrina.

"Excuse me . . . Pardon me . . . Ouch . . . Hey, watch the fin, buddy!" Sabrina finally managed to swim away. "Whoa. This fish business is harder than I thought. With the eels and the sharks, and . . . *SHARK!*"

A gigantic blue shark was swimming full speed in Sabrina's direction! She shot off for the protection of the coral reef, leaving a streak of bubbles behind her. She peeked out from behind a piece of staghorn coral, and gratefully saw the shark swim away.

"Whew. Two snaps away from being the catch of the day." Just as Sabrina was beginning to relax, a dolphin came from behind and flipped her up with his snout.

"*Whaaa . . .*"

Sabrina shot out of the water at incredible speed and spun through the air for what felt like forever. Just before she was about to crash back down, the playful dolphin caught her on his snout and balanced her like a ball.

"I'd be more upset if this didn't tickle so much," she said, beginning to laugh. The dolphin flipped her back up into the air, but this time, she landed with a very wet *splash!* She tumbled and rolled down through the water, spitting out saltwater along the way. Sabrina patted her middle with her fin and said, "I didn't know you could get seasick underwater." She looked up and saw the dolphin swimming toward her again, with a mischievous glint in his eye.

"Oh, no you don't!" she cried, magically turning herself back into a girl. The dolphin stopped and turned away, frightened.

"Bully," said Sabrina through her mouthpiece.

Gwen and the strange man were still floating next to each other near the inflatable Zodiac.

"I'm Barnaby," he said, treading water. His arms and chest were so muscular, it took her a few moments to pull her eyes away and respond.

"Gwen," she blurted out. *Two gorgeous guys in one day—my luck must be changing!*

As her eyes went back to those strong arms, she noticed a red swelling on his shoulder. "What happened? Did you brush up against some coral?"

"Ah, no," he said. "It's kind of why . . ."

Suddenly, Sabrina popped out of the water right next to Gwen. She pulled off her mouthpiece and mask, and said, "Gwen, you're not going to believe what I found."

"Sabrina, I want you to meet . . ." Gwen turned around, but Barnaby was gone! "Barnaby," she said, very flustered.

"Barnaby. Jerome. Aren't there any guys in England?" joked Sabrina.

"But he," began Gwen, scanning the open water for a sign of him.

". . . is probably really cute. Come on, we've got to find Dr. Martin," said Sabrina, diving back underwater.

A gentle breeze blew the white lace curtains open in Hillary's hotel room. A waiter entered and set a tray with a large silver cover on the table. "Anything else, Miss Hexton?"

Over the sound of running water, Hillary said sweetly from the bathroom, "No. Now be a good boy and toddle along." After the waiter left, Hillary emerged with a mud pack hardening on her face and bleach in her whiskers. She gracefully leapt up to the table, only slightly jarring her carefully placed shower cap. She eyed the silver tray happily, but before she had a chance to pull off the cover, Salem burst out!

"Surprise!" he said, prancing toward her.

"Aahh! What are you doing here?" she gasped, stepping backward.

"Aahh! What are you wearing?" he cried, getting an eyeful of hardened mud pack and bleach.

25

"Get out!" Hillary yelled, pointing to the door. Salem slipped off the table and out the door, his tail escaping certain death by milliseconds. *Slam!*

"I wish I could remember why that seemed like such a good idea," he muttered, slinking down the hall.

Sabrina and Gwen surfaced next to the Zodiac, where Dr. Martin was taking off his diving gear.

"Dr. Martin," said Sabrina. "I think I saw a *Chaetodon plebeius.*" Dr. Martin smiled as he helped them onto the boat.

"What? The blue-spot butterfly fish? Sabrina, that fish is . . ."

"Extinct. I know," she said, sitting down.

"Are you sure?" he asked.

"Yellow with a blue oval, vertical black band through the eye and mouth and a false eye on its tail," she replied matter-of-factly. Dr. Martin gazed down at her, impressed.

"I saw a bunch of shiny yellow ones," added Gwen. Dr. Martin laughed and as soon as everyone was back on board, he started the engine and set off for home.

Barnaby watched from a distance as the inflatable Zodiac sped toward shore. He raised his arm and gave a half-hearted wave, the sadness in his face reflected in the dark blue of the open sea.

Chapter 3

When they got back to shore, Dr. Martin invited Sabrina to his Marine Research Institute. They entered a big, open space lined with huge tanks full of exotic marine life. Tables and desks were cluttered with navigational maps, sea routes, and breathtaking pictures of underwater plants and animals. They stopped at Dr. Martin's desk, where he quickly turned on his computer, and began scanning his files.

A picture of a beautiful fish lit up the monitor. The translucent yellow of its body perfectly reflected the blue oval and black band that shot down through its eye and mouth. The fake eye on its tail hummed and glowed on the screen.

"Is this what you saw?" asked Dr. Martin.

"Exactly. Though he's surprisingly short in person," she added with a grin.

"Incredible. No one has seen that fish for fifty years. And I still can't figure out how you did. They live deep inside the reef. Never out in the open . . ." His eyes were full of questions.

"Guess this one got lost," she said quickly, looking away.

"We'll need to verify the sighting and register it with—" But before Dr. Martin could finish, his assistant came rushing into the room.

"Julian, we have another dolphin beached over in Paradise Cove. Looks fairly critical," he said grimly. Dr. Martin opened a cabinet near his desk. He pulled out some medical supplies and shoved them haphazardly inside his bag.

"What's wrong?" asked Sabrina.

"An abnormally high toxin level in the water on the other side of the island is causing some of the larger marine life to get sick and die."

"Die?" she gasped. "Isn't there anything you can do?"

"If we're lucky to find them early enough, we stand a good chance of saving them. But whales and dolphins aren't great about seeking medical attention." Sabrina followed him out the door and down toward the dock.

"They become weak," he continued, "and disoriented, and are susceptible to predators. It's usually accompanied by some kind of rash on their fins and tail."

"But what's causing it?" she asked, struggling to keep his pace.

"I'm fairly certain a ship has recently begun illegally dumping its waste into the ocean. But I have no proof. The resort is fanatical about prosecuting offenders, but it's almost impossible to catch them in the act." Dr. Martin shook his head sadly. "We'll talk more about your fish later," he said, hurrying to his boat.

Empty room-service trays and half-eaten jars of macadamia nuts littered the table in Salem's deluxe suite. He was lying on his back, desperately waiting for the phone to ring. Looking at it wasn't working. Angrily, he flicked his tail against the window, and the dark shade dropped down and obscured his stunning beach view. He let out a deep, pitiful sigh.

Brring! Brring!

"Hello? Hillary?" he cried into the speakerphone.

"No," said the manager, "I'm sorry, but Miss Hexton has sent back your very generous gift." The manager paused and stared at a bucket full of fresh fish. "I know it's none of my business, sir, but might I suggest, next time you try flowers . . ."

Salem groaned and covered his face with his paws.

Hilda and Zelda magically appeared, bikini-clad and freezing, on a bridge overlooking the Thames.

The great old clock, Big Ben, was across the river, and a gentle rain was falling over the gray city.

Zelda scowled and immediately pointed them into long pants and sweaters. "London!" she sniffed. "Really, Hilda, what were you thinking?"

"Hmm . . ." said Hilda, watching a red double-decker bus drive by on the wrong side of the road. "I must have gotten confused over the accent thing. Still," she added cheerfully, "I'm sure we could find a kangaroo somewhere so it's not a total wash—and I'm starved. Let's get some food."

A man in a trench coat carrying a black umbrella stopped in front of them. "I say," he said politely. "Are you ladies lost?"

Hilda smiled her most bewitching smile and said sweetly, "Are there any kangaroos nearby?"

The man paused, a bit taken aback. "Well," he said nervously, "there's always the zoo . . ."

"He left rather quickly, don't you think?" observed Zelda dryly, watching him hurry off.

Hilda shrugged, completely unfazed. "I could really go for a fresh, crunchy salad. Let's—"

"This is England, not California!" Zelda interrupted. "There are no fresh vegetables here—this is the home of canned peas, wilted lettuce and blood pudding. You don't come here to *eat*. Come on, I'm going to get us out of here."

"No!" said Hilda. "My mistake, let me fix it." She closed her eyes and pointed. "I'm visualizing hot sun, water, and"—she opened her eyes a crack to make sure Zelda wasn't peeking—"an international man of mystery."

Sabrina and Gwen met up for an afternoon walk down the beach. The sun was radiant, bouncing and sparkling off the clear sea. "What a smashing vacation this is turning out to be. You find a supposedly extinct fish and I might have a boyfriend. The odds of either are incredible," said Gwen. They looked at each other and burst out laughing.

I've flown through the universe, thought Sabrina, *hitched a ride on a shooting star and kissed Harvey Kinkel. But swimming underwater near the reefs— actually feeling the touch of a school of fish darting past—definitely an all-time high.* Sabrina walked a few steps ahead, and knelt down to inspect a bright blue shell.

When she looked up, something flickered in the water farther down the beach. The light was so intense, she had to shield her eyes from the reflection. "What's that?" she asked Gwen.

"Oh, no!" Gwen cried. "I think it's a dolphin." They ran down the beach, stunned to see a large tail covered in shiny scales moving in the shallow water. When they were a few yards away, they stopped dead in their tracks. The sparkling fish tail was the bottom half of a gorgeous guy!

"Gwen, it's not a dolphin . . ."

A merman?

"Barnaby!" Gwen cried, kneeling at his side. "Sabrina, it's the guy I was talking to on the reef. I had no idea he was a mer . . . man."

"The giant fish tail didn't make you suspicious? Help me try to find a pulse," said Sabrina, reaching for his wrist.

"What's the matter with him? Is he going to be all right?" asked Gwen. Sabrina laid her head on his chest and listened to his heartbeat.

"I don't know. But he's still breathing, or whatever it is merguys do. We've got to try and revive him somehow," said Sabrina thoughtfully. Gwen frantically splashed fistfuls of seawater on him. At least, it was *meant* for Barnaby. "Did that help?" she asked.

Sabrina shook the water off her face and hair. "Yeah, I was getting kind of hot. I was thinking more along the lines of mouth to gill resuscitation."

Out in the bay, a lovely mermaid and her dolphin friend were gazing sadly at the shore. Her long hair glowed in the gentle waves, spreading out around her like a glorious, sea-kissed mane.

"Spout," said the mermaid, "we're too late! Humans have him. What are we going to do?" Spout squeaked and shook his head sadly.

Sabrina knelt over Barnaby, her lips inches from his. She hesitated, and sat back down. "I don't know if we should be forcing water into his lungs or out of them. I really think he needs to be back in the water."

"We can't just roll him into the ocean," said Gwen. "He'll drown. Or maybe he's drowning now . . ."

Gwen looked up and saw some tourists heading down the beach. "People!" she cried.

"This might be a little difficult to explain," said Sabrina. Then she pointed and the three of them disappeared.

Far out in the bay, the mermaid and the dolphin gasped. "I didn't know they could do that," she said. Her voice quivered in fear.

The afternoon aerobics class was under way on the beach. Dozens of bikini-clad women were jumping up and down on exercise mats in the hot afternoon sun. "And a one, two, three, four," called the instructor, kicking her leg into the air with her arms raised high above her head.

Hillary was in the front row, sporting a headband and a black leotard. She raised her paw and kicked it gracefully into the air.

Salem was watching Hillary from beside the instructor's raised platform. "Me-*ow*," he murmured, gazing at her shapely legs rising and falling in perfect time.

He slinked toward her, leaping over several startled kicking women, and landed on her mat.

"Bewitched to see you again," he said with an exaggerated bow. Hillary was not amused. Salem planted himself firmly by her side, and started raising his paws in an aggressive attempt to outdo her. Sand flew everywhere, and so did his legs.

"Your form is awful," Hillary snapped, pausing to brush sand from her nose.

"On your back, ladies! And let's work those abs! And a one, two . . ." called the instructor.

Salem flipped onto his back and struggled to raise his head. Hillary was moving up and down like a well-oiled machine.

"Don't hurt yourself," she said slyly. Salem pushed himself up with all of his might, and collapsed into the sand, dazed.

After the sit-ups came push-ups, jogging in place, leg lifts and buttock rolls. Hillary turned to Salem. He had fallen into a deep sleep, muttering something about pain, women, and what had he done to deserve this.

"Well done, ladies! That's it for today." The instructor waved, still full of boundless energy, and jogged off down the beach.

Hillary leaned down, her whiskers inches from Salem's panting mouth. "Well done, ladies," she said with a smirk. She jumped up and quickly dried herself off with a towel. Then, she flicked her tail suggestively down his furry tummy, threw her wet towel on top of him and walked away without a backward glance.

Salem held her towel close, inhaling her intoxicating scent. *Definitely interested. Can't keep her tail off me . . .*

Sabrina, Gwen and the still unconscious Barnaby appeared in Sabrina's bungalow. "Help me get him into the tub," said Sabrina, grabbing hold of his tail. Gwen struggled with his arms, and together they stumbled toward the bathroom.

Just then, a maid came out of the room and saw the gigantic, shimmering fish tail. *"Aahh!"* she screamed.

Sabrina wiped sweat off her brow and said, "I was right, it is difficult to explain." Gwen, in panic mode, clenched her fist and the maid was suddenly drenched with water.

"What exactly have you been practicing? The piano?" Sabrina asked. She tossed a sheet over Barnaby. "You really should get someone to look at that air conditioner. It's been dripping all day," she called to the maid.

Sabrina and Gwen quickly backed out of the room and down the steps. The upper half of Barnaby's body was still covered with a sheet, but the huge fish tail was glowing in the sun for everyone to see.

They carried Barnaby up the pathway past some bungalows and a group of large palm trees. They turned a corner and nearly walked right into two fishermen, who were on their way up the path from the dock. They stared in disbelief at the enormous fish.

"Pretty amazing, huh?" said Sabrina. "Just a hot dog and a piece of string . . ." She and Gwen disappeared around the bend, leaving the stunned fishermen shaking their heads.

Chapter 4

Salem was lying on a bench on the resort grounds, enjoying the shade of a nearby tree. The beach spread out before him, dotted with palm trees and colorful beach umbrellas. A stack of postcards and pens lay by his side. He had already written most of his friends and acquaintances, reminding them all of how much they must miss him, but advising them to remain strong, for he would be among them soon enough . . . He pulled a card from the pile, settled in on the bench and began to read aloud. "Dear Aunt Eunice, having a wonderful time. Thrilled you're not here." He smiled smugly at his wit, and prepared to read another card, when an outrageously large fish tail fell onto the ground in front of him. Salem's eyes popped wide open and a delicious smile crossed his furry face. "My kingdom for a sushi chef . . ."

Sabrina bent down and tried to pick up the unwieldy tail. "Sabrina, be careful," admonished Gwen. Sabrina shrugged. "He's slippery . . ."

Salem sat upright. "Sabrina?"

She turned around. "Salem?" Baranaby's tail hit the ground with a thud. *Oh, nooo!* thought Sabrina. She loved her cat familiar, and listening to his complaints at home was one thing—but on vacation?! Major bum-out.

Salem smirked. "Nice fish."

Moments later, Sabrina and Gwen, still carrying the unconscious Barnaby, burst into Salem's room. It looked like a tornado had hit the deluxe suite. Room-service trays, dirty towels, candy wrappers and old magazines were strewn everywhere.

"Hurry," said Sabrina. "We've got to get him into some water." Salem ran into the room and jumped onto the unmade bed. "This better not take long," he complained. "I've got a massage in twenty minutes."

Sabrina glared sullenly at Salem. His yellow eyes responded with a what-did-I-do-to-deserve-this look. She sighed. He was the same as always—king of the self-centered cats. Finally, Sabrina and Gwen managed to get Barnaby into the tub. Suddenly, water poured out of the shower head. "Aahh!" cried Sabrina, drenched. "That's the shower!"

* * *

Hillary peeked her perfectly coifed head through the open door. "Hello? Salem?" she purred.

"Hillary!" he exclaimed, delighted.

"I wanted to apologize for earlier. My therapist says I can be a little judgmental. And you seem like a decent, flea-free guy . . ."

"I'll get the magic book," called Gwen, darting past the talking cats and out the front door.

"Salem," cried Sabrina, peeking out from the bathroom, "I need salt! Lots of it."

". . . who has a room full of women . . ." finished Hillary, bewildered.

Sabrina ran to the room-service trays and scooped up all of the saltshakers.

Salem shrugged. "There's a very simple explanation—"

"Wow!" said Sabrina. "This place is even messier than your room at home. I hope this is enough. Does it sound like the water's overflowing?"

"—just not one I can think of at the moment," finished Salem, trying to regain his dignity.

Sabrina reached over Hillary for the last of the saltshakers. "Excuse me," she said pleasantly.

"Not a problem. I was just leaving." Hillary scampered out the door, with Salem trailing behind her.

Sabrina balanced the saltshakers in her arms. "A random talking cat. I'd be a little more curious if I didn't have an unconscious merman in the bathtub." Sabrina hurried back into the bathroom and emptied the saltshakers into the tub. She gently mixed the salt water with her hands, trying to cover all of Barnaby's tail.

"I've got it," cried Gwen, running into the bathroom carrying the magic book. "There's a whole chapter on sea creatures."

Sabrina and Gwen were kneeling by the tub, pouring water over Baranby, when Salem charged in and jumped onto the hamper.

"Well." He glared. "I hope you're happy! I can't believe you'd come halfway around the world to destroy my vacation."

"I came halfway around the world to get away from you."

"Don't try to sweet-talk me now," he snarled.

"I thought you took your vacation on Nantucket," said Sabrina, massaging Barnaby's arms.

"That's just what I tell people. I value my privacy."

"So do I! That's why I've been talking about coming here for months. I even gave you a book to read about this place."

Salem scowled. "Oh. Never read it."

"At least I'm not the only one," said Gwen.

"But," added Salem, "I am using it to press flowers. Now, kindly get the comatose fish boy out of my tub and get off my island."

"Your island!" cried Sabrina. "I should . . ." Barnaby's tail began to flap.

"He's waking up!" said Gwen. "The salt water

is working." Barnaby's tail twisted and turned, and his eyes popped open. "Aahh!" he yelled. "Who are you? Where am I?" His tail flicked with incredible speed, sending torrents of water everywhere.

"Calm down," said Sabrina. "And quit splashing." Barnaby flailed his body helplessly in the tub.

"He's getting water everywhere!" snapped Salem.

More water sloshed out of the tub. "Your animal," said Barnaby. "It talks!"

Sabrina rolled her eyes. *And I still can't believe he's here—major pain!* "Yeah, but he never really has anything to say."

"Barnaby," said Gwen. "Don't you remember me? Gwen. We met on the reef."

"Oh yeah. Startled to see you again," he said, beginning to calm down.

"We're trying to help you," explained Sabrina. "We found you washed up on the beach and brought you back to our tub."

"My tub," added Salem. "Which now smells like old tuna."

"Last thing I remember," said Barnaby, "is being chased by a boat. Normally, I'd have no trouble getting away, but I've been so tired . . ."

"Why were you even swimming around out here?" asked Gwen. "I thought mythical creatures were supposed to keep hidden."

Salem grinned. "Ask any unicorn."

"Actually, it's forbidden to have contact with leg walkers," said Barnaby. "Humans. But you're my last hope. I was going to ask Gwen for help, but then I got scared when she showed up. I tried again with the next group I found, but they weren't as nice."

"It's about your shoulder, isn't it?" asked Sabrina. The swollen rash on his shoulder was getting worse, and there were some nasty bruises down his arm. "It looks like some sort of fungus."

"I thought it was a bruise," said Gwen.

"No," said Sabrina. "He's got some on his tail, too. Do you live on the other side of the island?"

Barnaby nodded.

"Sabrina, how do you know all this?" asked Gwen.

"It's got to be the same thing that Dr. Martin was telling me about. He has all the symptoms. Barnaby, if we don't treat this right away it can be—"

". . . fatal. I know," finished Barnaby. "That's why I didn't think I had anything to lose."

"We have to find a way to get Dr. Martin to look at him," said Sabrina.

"I might not have noticed the tail at first, but I'm pretty sure that Dr. Martin will. He is a scientist, after all," said Gwen.

Sabrina picked up the magic book. "Unless . . ." She and Gwen looked at each other in silence.

"What?" asked Barnaby.

Sabrina took a deep breath. "Barnaby, the rest of

the world probably won't be as comfortable with your tail as we are."

"But," added Gwen, "there might be a way that we can . . . change it."

"There are a lot of different forces that make up the universe . . ." said Sabrina.

"Some things can't easily be explained," Gwen continued.

"And while we may seem like normal, everyday leg walkers, we're . . ."

". . . unique," finished Gwen.

Barnaby stared at them both, completely baffled.

Salem, completely irritated, blurted out, "Oh, for the love a . . . They're witches!"

"Salem!" said Sabrina sternly.

"Witches?" Barnaby sputtered. "Right. What do you take me for? A sea slug? Even I know that witches don't exist."

Sabrina pointed and the bathroom dried instantly. "For a guy with a tail, you're extremely narrow-minded."

Moments later, Sabrina and Gwen were sitting on Salem's unmade bed, flipping through the magic book. "Serpents, sea monsters, sirens, a recipe for bouillabaisse . . ."

"There!" pointed Gwen. "Mermaids . . . I don't know about this one, Sabrina. There's no reversing spell."

"Sabrina!" Barnaby called from the bathroom. "Hurry up . . . I don't like the way your cat is looking at me." Barnaby's tail was flopped over the side of the tub, flipping nervously.

"Maybe broiled with a little garlic butter. No, smothered in cornbread batter and deep fried . . ." Salem licked his lips, his eyes wide with desire.

"Look!" wailed Barnaby as Sabrina and Gwen came into the bathroom. "He's starting to foam at the mouth."

"Actually," drawled Salem, *"he's* been eating soap." Barnaby nodded and held up a bar of soap with a big bite mark. "Kind of tastes like starfish."

"It's not for eating," said Sabrina. "I found a spell that will give you legs for forty-eight hours."

"Really? Legs? You mean like the two of you?"

Salem snorted. "Hopefully not *just* like the two of them or you'll be headlining in the Sydney production of *Victor/Victoria.*"

"Once we change you," said Gwen, "the spell can't be reversed. You have to let it run its course."

"So?" said Barnaby. "I always wondered what it would be like to have legs. I'm ready when you are."

Sabrina opened the magic book and flipped through until she found the spell. She was just about to start the incantation, when she said to Gwen, "Give him a towel."

"Spoil sport," Gwen muttered, handing one to Barnaby.

Sabrina pointed at Barnaby's tail and said, *"Water and sand / land and air / Give me a man, with legs to spare . . ."* A soft glowing haze covered Barnaby's tail. The scales flickered and sparkled and unraveled into two muscular legs. Barnaby stood up in the tub, delighted. "Look at me!" he cried. "I'm standing!"

"Oh, sure," grumbled Salem. "The fish gets to be a man, but the cat, no."

☆

Chapter 5

☆

Splash! Sabrina's aunts tumbled headfirst into a pond of shallow water. Hilda sat up, wiped her eyes and looked around. Beautifully manicured grass sprawled out before them, interspersed with small ponds and clusters of lush trees. She sighed. *I can just imagine the ocean waves flowing past those sloping hills . . .*

A bird swooped down in the soft grass nearby. "Look, Zelda! A seagull—"

"That's not a seagull," interrupted Zelda. "It's a robin. And this," she added, pulling a golf ball out of her pocket, "is not something normally found on a beach."

Hilda pouted. "Well, what on Earth," she said, staring off into the distance. A group of men carrying golf clubs had appeared on top of a hill.

46

"Duck!" cried Zelda. "Incoming!" Two golf balls whirled past their heads at amazing speed.

"You have taken us to a water trap on a golf course," Zelda sputtered. "What is *with* your sense of direction?"

Before Hilda could respond, a golf cart pulled up by the pond. The driver flashed them a brilliant smile as he pushed up his black sunglasses. He had on a bright green shirt and even brighter red pants.

"What did you conjure?" snapped Zelda. "A golf pro?"

"All right, all right," grumbled Hilda. "My magic seems a bit off today . . ." She pointed and the man and his golf cart vanished instantly.

"I get that he was a man, and that he well may have been mysterious, but how was he international?" asked Hilda.

Zelda rolled her eyes. "Goofballs come in every nationality."

"I'll get it right this time—third time's the charm," said Hilda, not at all sure that was true . . .

Barnaby, with Sabrina and Gwen by his side, was taking his first tentative steps on the resort grounds. In his sleeveless T-shirt, hot yellow shorts and dark sunglasses, he looked like your everyday drop-dead gorgeous surfer guy. A drop-dead gorgeous surfer guy who was just learning to walk, that is.

"They might look ridiculous, but they seem to work pretty well," he said, pointing at his two muscular legs. He put his hands on the sides of his shorts, and some of his fingers slipped into a pocket. Barnaby laughed, and shoved both hands inside.

"What are they?" he asked, amazed.

"Pockets," said Sabrina. "You put things in them, like keys, gum . . ." Barnaby found a nearby garbage can full of . . . well . . . garbage. Delighted, he shoved a banana peel, bits of old newspaper, and an empty soda can into his pockets.

". . . garbage," finished Sabrina with a grin.

Barnaby stopped walking and stared at the resort grounds. The pathway was wide, shaded by lush, green plants towering from above. There were palm trees with their long, narrow leaves and tall, spiky barks. There were coconut trees and pineapple trees heavy with fruit. Colorful birds of paradise stared majestically from the branches, blinking wisely at passersby. There was a rustle in the low brush, and two baby wallabies peeked through. Barnaby laughed, delighted, as they pinched up their little noses and hopped away. "This is the most incredible place I've ever seen," he said softly.

Farther down, the pathway widened and was buzzing with activity. People in all shapes and sizes were walking, bike riding, rollerblading, and jogging. A bicyclist rode nearby, and Barnaby, enthralled, jumped in front of him. The bicyclist shouted obscenities, swerving out of the way just in time. Barnaby smiled sweetly after him. "You probably don't need to add any of those words to your vocabulary," said Sabrina, shaking her head.

Barnaby leapt forward and ran down the path toward the beach. A relaxed volleyball game was under way, and the players were laughing and joking in the deep afternoon sun.

Barnaby jumped eagerly into the game and caught the ball. He smiled, delighted by its weight and texture, and held it to his ear.

"Look!" he cried to Sabrina and Gwen, who were running up to him. The volleyball players demanded their ball back, and circled Barnaby angrily. Panting, Sabrina caught up to him and grabbed the ball. "Sorry," she explained. "Surfer, one too many boogie boards to the head." She threw the ball back to them and dragged Barnaby back to the path. He resisted, and pushed them away. "Wait," he said. "What's the . . ."

"Be fascinated in this direction," said Sabrina, pointing to a sign down the beach that said MARINE RESEARCH INSTITUTE.

The mermaid and Spout swam close to the shore, scanning the resort and the beach for signs of Barnaby. Spout squeaked loudly and jumped up in the water, pointing straight ahead with his fin. Barnaby and the two girls were walking along the water's edge toward the Research Institute.

The mermaid gasped. "What have they done to him? They've turned him into some kind of mutant." Spout plunged into the water and headed for the beach.

"Spout, no!" she cried. "Come back!" But the dark outline of his body moved silently toward shore.

The three of them walked along the beach, dipping their feet into the cool water as the tide came in. Suddenly, Spout slid out of the water, and threw himself on the sand in front of Sabrina.

Sabrina and Gwen cried out, amazed, and grabbed each other's hands. "Spout!" said Barnaby. He knelt down and gave the dolphin a big hug.

"This is Spout," said Barnaby. "Spout, this is Sabrina and Gwen." Sabrina's eyes narrowed in recognition and she clasped her sore rib. "We've met," she said. "Hi."

"Pleasure," said Gwen, laughing as Spout rolled happily back and forth on the warm sand.

Barnaby grinned. "I know, they're pretty cute." Spout squeaked in agreement, and then started squeaking in a serious tone.

"What?" asked Barnaby. "Fin?" Troubled, he looked out at the bay. Spout rolled back into the water and disappeared in the waves. Barnaby walked a few feet into the sea, enjoying the new sensation of his cold feet touching the moist sand. The mermaid swam close to the shore, but kept her distance.

"It's my sister, Fin," he explained. Barnaby lifted

his leg toward Fin and said, "Look. Aren't they great?"

Fin scowled. "They're disgusting. Make them change you back. I can't even stand to look at you."

Barnaby sighed. "Fin, come on. Be reasonable. They're just trying to help." Fin shook her head and after a long, concerned look, dove far into the sea.

Barnaby sat at the water's edge, the waves gently splashing his legs. "Sorry you had to hear that," he said sadly. "She's not the biggest fan of humans."

"I know if I suddenly saw my brother with legs I'd be a little upset, too," said Gwen, ignoring Sabrina's raised eyebrows. "Currently he's a tree. Don't ask. Mum still hasn't forgiven me."

Sabrina waded through the water and took Barnaby's hand. "Maybe she'll change her opinion once we get you to a doctor." She helped him stand up, and the three of them continued walking toward the Research Institute.

Inside the Research Institute, Dr. Martin and his assistant were sitting at his desk flipping through photographs. "What is this?" demanded Dr. Martin. "Some kind of joke?" The photograph showed a glittering mermaid's tail breaking a wave. Another picture revealed a shadowy image of a merman swimming just below the surface.

"It's not a joke," said his assistant. "I took the pictures myself. We were out looking for your blue-spot butterfly fish, when this thing just appeared."

Dr. Martin stroked his chin. "It's got to be some play of light, a dolphin . . ."

"It's not a dolphin. We chased it for over half an hour."

"Where do you think it was heading?" asked Dr. Martin, carefully studying the photographs.

His assistant shrugged. "No idea. Could be anywhere."

"I don't know if somebody's having a huge laugh at our expense, or we really have . . . mermaids swimming around out there. But I'll tell you one thing," said Dr. Martin, his fist hitting the table, "I'm going to find it."

"Excuse me, Dr. Martin?"

Dr. Martin and his assistant spun around. Sabrina, Gwen and Barnaby were standing in the open door.

Chapter 6

Barnaby was sitting on a cluttered desk in the Research Institute. He glanced wearily at Dr. Martin, who was carefully examining his shoulder.

"Do you have this anywhere else?" asked Dr. Martin.

Barnaby tensed. "There's some on my tail." Sabrina gasped and said quickly, "Bone. His tail bone and some on his legs."

Dr. Martin bent down and studied Barnaby's legs and lower back. "I don't believe it, but I think you might be right, Sabrina." Dr. Martin went over to a high-powered microscope and looked inside.

Barnaby jumped down from the desk and riffled through a stack of papers. Gwen grabbed them, carefully putting them back in order just as Barnaby dumped a jar of paper clips onto the floor.

"It appears to be almost identical to what's been affecting the marine mammals," said Dr. Martin, his eyes still glued to the microscope.

Gwen rushed down to the floor and wrestled the paper clips away from Barnaby.

"Great," said Sabrina. "Because you said you were able to treat it, right? If you caught it early enough."

Dr. Martin looked up. "I said we've had some success with dolphins and whales . . ."

"But if it's the same disease," said Sabrina, "wouldn't it work on a mer . . . hu . . . Barnaby?" Dr. Martin wasn't listening. He was studying the microscope intently.

After Barnaby kindly helped Gwen put all the paper clips back into the jar, he noticed a ball-point pen on the table. Intrigued, he started sniffing and tasting it. Gwen tried to take it away, but he held it high over her head, laughing as she tried to grab it.

"If this is beginning to affect humans . . . But why haven't we seen it before?" said Dr. Martin, his voice muffled through the microscope.

"So, what do you use? An ointment? A shot? Antibiotics?" asked Sabrina.

"What?" said Dr. Martin, clearly distracted.

Sabrina sighed. "To cure it."

Dr. Martin looked up. "An ointment." He walked over to a locked cabinet, unlocked it, and pulled out a small plastic bottle.

"Then let's try it and see if it works," said Sabrina. "If it does, great. If it doesn't, well, let's hope it does. Remember, you said you had to catch it early."

"Sabrina!" cried Gwen, from the other side of the room. Sabrina and Dr. Martin rushed over. Barnaby was shaking his head uncontrollably. His face had contorted horribly and his tongue darted in and out of his mouth.

"Barnaby?" said Sabrina, a little frightened.

"I think I have some water in my ear," he said. Then, he turned his head and started banging the other side, trying to shake the water out.

Sabrina laughed nervously. "Swimmer's ear. Always in the water. Probably how he got this in the first place—"

Woosh!

Suddenly, twenty gallons of water poured out of Barnaby's ear! It flowed, no, it rushed, down the table, over some files, charts and graphs until it formed a small lake near a fish tank. No one said a word.

"Whew," said Barnaby, smiling broadly. "That's better." Sabrina and Gwen exchanged a long look. Sabrina took a deep breath and pointed. "Would you look at that. You've got a leak in one of your fish tanks . . ."

The tank beside Barnaby was leaking quickly onto the floor.

"But . . ." said Dr. Martin, stunned.

"Well, thanks for taking a look at him," said Sabrina, grabbing the ointment from his hand. "Really appreciate it. Gotta go." She pushed Gwen and Barnaby toward the door. She looked back at Dr. Martin and said, "Oh, you might want to . . ." She held up her fingers and mimed plugging up the hole.

Dr. Martin, completely perplexed, stuck his finger into the tiny hole in the fish tank.

Sabrina and Gwen finally managed to hustle Barnaby out of the Research Institute. It was no easy task; he was distracted by the sliding doors, the blue carpet near the exit, and the flashing computer screens.

"Well," said Sabrina, "that went well, at least until you turned into a giant fountain . . ."

Dr. Martin had patched up the fish tank with some very strong black tape. He was sitting at his desk, studying the photographs with a magnifying glass when his assistant walked in.

"Are you sure whatever you saw had a tail?" asked Dr. Martin, his eyes glued to the picture.

"Positive. You've got the picture. Why?"

Dr. Martin passed him the photo of the merman swimming underwater. "There's some discoloration on the left shoulder. They're almost identical to the marks on the guy Sabrina just brought in . . ."

His assistant stared at him, speechless.

* * *

Hillary and Salem were sitting side by side at the beach bar, sipping fruit smoothies. "Against my better judgment, I'll believe your story and accept your apology," she purred.

"Thank you," said Salem.

Hillary leaned in close. "Besides, I'm bored out of my whiskers and you're the only other talking cat on this rock."

"In other words, beggars can't be choosers," he observed dryly.

"Correct." She smiled, grabbing a pawful of nuts.

"Yes!" he grinned. "I knew you'd come around."

Barnaby and Sabrina were lounging on the deck of her bungalow. The ocean was a few yards away, and the sea air smelled like tropical perfume. The wind rustled the leaves of the palm trees overhead, creating a cool breeze. She was sitting behind him, gently rubbing the ointment onto his shoulder.

"Once every two hours, and by tomorrow, you'll be as good as new," she said, giving him an extra pat on the back for reassurance.

Gwen joined them on the deck, wearing her bathing suit and a towel wrapped around her middle. "Mind if I pop out for a bit? I'm finally going to get that windsurfing lesson."

Sabrina laughed as Gwen waved good-bye.

Barnaby turned to face Sabrina. "Do I have to sit in here to make this stuff work?"

"I don't think so, why?"

He smiled brightly. "Because I've got legs and forty-eight hours to use 'em . . ."

Later that afternoon, Sabrina was racing through the water on a wave runner. Her blond hair was flying in the wind and the spray from the boat cooled her from the sun's glare. She turned to watch Barnaby skidding behind on his water skis, laughing. He brought a hand up and waved, when he suddenly lost his balance. Concerned, Sabrina slowed the boat down. Barnaby regained his equilibrium and sliced his skis upward, spraying her with water as he shot ahead of the boat. Sabrina shook her head in amazement, and sped after him . . .

A CD playing the sounds of a gentle rain was piped into the Health Spa's rest and relaxation room. A masseur and masseuse worked intently on their clients, who were lying facedown on side-by-side tables. "Oh, my . . ." purred Hillary. Salem groaned in pure ecstasy.

Once Sabrina got Barnaby on water skis, it was nearly impossible to get him off them—but she promised him that his next adventure would be just as fun. After some drying off, they headed up to the Resort Shop. Barnaby was like a kid in a toy store. His eyes widened when he saw the stuffed koala bears and kangaroos, the Australian flags, Hamilton Island T-shirts and monogrammed mugs. He was delighted with everything; he dragged Sabrina through the store, demanding explanations for stuffed cockatoos, multicolored key chains, and Gummy Bears shaped like fish. *Gummy Bears shaped like fish,* thought Sabrina. *Try explaining that one to a merman!*

Later that afternoon, Sabrina was in the water, showing off her perfect crawl stroke. Barnaby tried his best to master it, but he couldn't quite figure out how to kick instead of flip. Farther out in the water, Gwen was getting her first windsurfing lesson. Jerome had instructed her on the importance of balancing properly, the best way to uphaul a sail and how to steer against an upwind. Gwen enjoyed listening to his adorable accent, but since she hated lessons of any kind and couldn't understand half of what he said, paid little attention. It showed. Each time she tried to get onto the board and stand up, she flipped right off, spraying water everywhere . . .

After Barnaby had exhausted himself with his first swimming lesson, Sabrina took him back to the resort dining room for an early dinner. The dining room had large windows that overlooked the bay, with an elaborate buffet set up on the other side. Barnaby dashed to the buffet, his mouth watering at the new sights and smells. He grabbed a handful of broccoli with cheese sauce, took a bite, and spit it out, disgusted. He accepted some medium-rare steak from a man wearing a long white hat. He took a tentative bite, and spit it right back out. The chef gasped in horror. Sabrina quickly rushed over, carrying a plate. *Mental note: If you're ever on a date with a merman, stay close by and always carry a plate!*

Salem and Hillary were asleep on their favorite spot on the beach, curled up against each other on a large blanket. A waiter was fanning them from behind, rolling his eyes at the absurdity of it all . . .

After dinner, Sabrina and Barnaby walked to the top of Lookout Point and watched the sun set over the restless sea. Pink and yellow clouds dotted the sky and cast a shimmering glow over the water. Barnaby had never seen anything like this before.

"I never knew any place could be so beautiful," he said quietly.

"I felt the same way when I went diving this morning," said Sabrina. They stared into each other's eyes and smiled . . .

That evening, Sabrina, Gwen and Barnaby were sitting at a table in the resort's night club. A banner hung from the stage that read TALENT SHOW. A group of guys in Hawaiian shirts had just finished singing, and were bowing to a smattering of applause.

Sabrina was wearing a black miniskirt and a black halter top that showed off her glowing tan.

Her blond hair was pulled back by a pink shell barrette. Gwen wore her skintight red slip dress. Sabrina looked at Gwen's outfit and thought, *Yup, she's definitely got it bad.*

Sabrina leaned close to Gwen. "Did he tell you what he was going to do?"

Gwen smiled nervously. "No, he just said he was going to sing."

The emcee took the microphone and said in a deep voice, "And our final contestant for the evening, all the way from Melbourne, Jerome Hester, The Singing Sea Maiden . . ." The spotlight darted stage left, and out pranced Jerome. His legs were wrapped in a sequined plastic tail and he was holding a ukulele. His eyes and lips were heavily made up, and as he waddled over to the microphone there was amused applause.

"Aunt Tutsi?!" cried Barnaby, jumping up. Sabrina and Gwen managed to pull him back down, just in time for Jerome to belt out "My Bonnie Lies Over the Ocean."

"My bonnie lies over the ocean, My bonnie lies over the sea . . ." he crooned to the appreciative crowd.

A little while later, Jerome flopped down at their table, proudly displaying his trophy. His smile was bigger than huge, and Gwen gazed at him, her eyes bursting with pride.

"Congratulations," Gwen gushed.

"Thanks," said Jerome. "Care to dance with a mer . . . man?"

"I'd love to," Gwen said, standing up. Barnaby stood up as well, thinking she meant *him* and offered Gwen his arm. Sabrina quickly grabbed it and said, "And I'll dance with Barnaby."

The dance floor was packed. They pushed through the crowd and started dancing. Jerome spun Gwen round and round as they laughed, improvising dips and turns along the way. Barnaby and Sabrina were holding hands, swaying gently to the music, when Barnaby started to really *feel* the rhythm. *Here we go . . .* Sabrina thought, as she was scooped up in two very powerful arms and tossed over his head and down and underneath and then back over again. A small crowd had gathered next to them, laughing and applauding. Finally, Sabrina disentangled herself and watched him dance around the crowd, undulating, and flapping his arms. *He still needs to work on those leg moves,* she thought to herself with a smile.

Chapter 7

After dancing, Sabrina and Barnaby left the night club and strolled down to the beach. The stars lit up the night sky, casting a soft glow on the liquid blue sea. Barnaby was ravenously eating his first dish of ice cream. "What do you call this stuff again?" he asked, licking the spoon.

Sabrina smiled. "Ice cream."

"It's great. Better than squid guts," he said, taking her hand and leading her down to the water's edge. The beach was empty and quiet. The only sounds were the waves washing the shore and the boats swaying in the evening tide. The lights from the re-sort reflected off the water like stars. *This must be paradise,* thought Sabrina. *And I'm sharing it with a guy who's about to lose his legs in thirty-six hours!*

Barnaby took both of her hands in his much

larger ones, and said softly, "Thank you for everything, Sabrina. Today has really been . . . magical."

She looked deeply into his beautiful, sea-colored eyes. "I was just thinking the same thing."

Barnaby smiled down at her. "What?" she asked.

"I don't know how humans show affection. We touch tails when we want to show that we care for someone."

"We hug, you know, put our arms around each other," said Sabrina, her arms reaching up around his shoulders. "Or we kiss . . ."

"Kiss?" asked Barnaby.

Sabrina laughed. "We touch our lips together."

"Really," said Barnaby, with a disgusted expression.

"I guess it doesn't sound quite as romantic when you have to explain it," she said, amused.

"Do you have someone back home you do that with?" he asked.

Sabrina nodded and moved her arms down to her side. "Yeah. I do."

"He's very lucky," said Barnaby.

"Thanks. And trust me, the kissing part grows on you . . ." *It sure does!* she thought, *and I know what I'd be doing right now if Harvey was by my side . . .*

Suddenly, Spout burst out of a large wave and landed on the beach in front of them.

"Spout!" cried Barnaby happily. "You're not

going to believe the day I had. It's been—"

Spout interrupted with a few loud squeaks and flipped his tail up for emphasis.

"What?" asked Barnaby, his smile fading instantly. "How bad?" Spout squeaked loudly a few more times.

"What's the matter?" asked Sabrina. "What's he squeaking?"

Barnaby turned to her, his face drawn and pale. "It's Fin. She's sick. I am such a barnacle sometimes. Here I am only thinking of myself, running around on these stupid . . ." He gestured to his legs. "I've got to go to her." He walked quickly into the water.

"Barnaby!" Sabrina cried.

He turned back and faced her. "But I can't swim. Sabrina, you have to change me back, now."

"Barnaby, I can't. The spell won't reverse itself for another thirty-six hours. I'm sorry . . ."

Barnaby plopped down in the sand.

"But," said Sabrina, "the medicine worked on you, it should work on her as well."

He shook his head sadly. "She'll never come here."

Sabrina took a deep breath. "What if I took it to her?"

"You'd do that? Oh, Sabrina, thank you!" He jumped up and hugged her. She suddenly tensed up.

"What's the matter?" he asked. "Aren't I doing it right?"

She nodded. "No, you're fine. But I think you just poured ice cream down my back . . ."

Hillary sighed, gazing out the large picture window in her hotel room. The stars glowed in the night sky and flickered romantically off the dark sea. She and Salem were curled together on a zebra-striped throw on top of her magnificent bed.

Salem dropped pieces of buttered popcorn into her mouth, as they watched *Catsablanca* on the television by the bed.

"This is so romantic," Hillary purred, resting her head against his shoulder. Salem leaned in for a kiss. "Play it again, Sam," she murmured with a satisfied smile.

Hilda and Zelda reappeared on a gondola, gently floating down a canal. Streams of tourists were walking down narrow streets and passing by on gondolas of their own, gazing at the magnificent beauty spread out before them. Zelda let out a contented sigh. "Even if there's not a dolphin in sight, I'll take Venice any day," she said dreamily.

Zelda zapped colorful sundresses on them, and a camcorder magically appeared in her hand. "Smile, dear. You look lovely," she said, turning on the camcorder and filming Hilda's glowing smile.

"Ah . . . we're passing under The Bridge of Sighs," she said softly. To their left was a breathtaking view of the lagoon, and the island of St. Giorgio, and then, darkness under the stone bridge. "The bridge got this name because in the seventeenth century—do listen up, Hilda, learning something new won't actually *hurt* you," reprimanded Zelda. "Ah, where was I? Yes, in the seventeenth century, the prisoner's last view of freedom was from this bridge. From here they were taken to their cells on the other side," she finished, pointing to the dark stone building.

Hilda sighed herself, starting to feel restless. "Let's do something," she said, sounding a little more bored than she meant to.

"Well . . . we could walk around the Piazza San Marco—the most famous square in Venice," suggested Zelda.

"Great," said Hilda, and with a quick point, they found themselves sitting in an outdoor café, two thick and frothy cappuccinos waiting for them on the table.

"Ah," said Zelda, gazing around her. "They call this the drawing room of the world. And it's still the central meeting place in all of Venice. Look around carefully and take notes—you may be able to use some of this in your next romantic fantasy . . ."

Hilda rolled her eyes and ordered some tiramisu from a waiter. It was around that time when she first noticed the birds. She spooned the creamy chocolate into her mouth and was sighing with pleasure, her favorite state to be in, when the first pigeon appeared. He seemed harmless at first. *What's the big deal about a pigeon,* she thought.

But, as Zelda was droning on and on about how all the historic periods were reflected in the architecture of the Ducal Palace, and pointing out the Gothic this and the Renaissance that, it seemed to her that the pigeon had magically cloned itself to the *n*th degree!

They were surrounded by pigeons! Pigeons underfoot, under the table, hopping on the empty chairs beside them. Zelda was oblivious to it all, still gazing up at the square, now going on about famous Renaissance painters.

Until a pigeon flew by her face and took a hearty gulp of the frothy cream in her cup.

"Yuck!" she screamed, standing up and shaking the table. Hilda jumped right up with her. They ran out of the café and through the square, pigeons flying and waddling after them eagerly.

"I feel like the Pied Piper of pigeons," said Zelda, scurrying down a narrow alley.

"I don't know about you, but I've had about enough of this," said Hilda, shooing away the pesky birds. She looked at her finger, and at Zelda. "Well, I hope my magic doesn't get even more messed up because I'm in a hurry, but, here goes . . ."

The sisters vanished, leaving hundreds of Italian pigeons cooing loudly after them.

The pink-fingered dawn was just rising over the water. The birds were singing their morning song and the trees were shaking out the evening's fragrant dampness. Sabrina was already up and dressed (if you call throwing a big T-shirt over a bathing suit dressed) and she was shaking Gwen out of what looked like a very pleasant dream. Gwen mumbled something about Jerome, the stars and pineapple smoothies and rolled over to go back to sleep. Sabrina had to steal her pillow and her covers before Gwen even opened one eye. It was a very irritated eye. Grumbling and complaining, Gwen threw on the clothes that Sabrina gave her, and followed her out the door.

They walked up the beach to the Marine Research Institute, and stopped in front of the gate.

"Maybe I should just tell Dr. Martin about Barnaby. You know he'd do everything he could to help," said Sabrina, shifting the waterproof, neoprene bag on her shoulder.

"And how are you going to explain the legs?" asked Gwen. "It would be the same as telling him you're a witch. You can't."

Sabrina sighed. "I know. Get Barnaby and I'll meet you at the dock." She slipped through the gate and into the building.

The room was empty and quiet except for the hum of the computers. She looked around until she saw a locked cabinet with the ointment visible inside. She studied the lock. "Shoot. There goes the, 'it just fell into my bag' excuse."

She looked around once more to make sure no

one was there, and then she pointed at the lock. The cabinet creaked open. She grabbed some ointment and quickly put it into her bag. She reached up to close the cabinet, when she saw Dr. Martin's face reflected in the glass.

"Aahh!" she screamed. "Dr. Martin, you're up early. I needed a little bit more of that ointment . . ."

His face was cold. "I can see that. Your friend still sick?"

"No, he's a lot better. But I found a dolphin that I thought could use it."

"A dolphin?" he said sarcastically. "They're seeking you out for medical advice now? If other things are coming down with this . . ." He sighed and added gently, "I wish you felt like you could trust me, Sabrina."

She looked away. "I do trust you. It's just . . . I wouldn't do this if it weren't really important."

"Well, we don't want any sick dolphins swimming around out there, but . . ." he reached for her bag and she instinctively pulled it back. ". . . I think I have a little more in my office," he finished. Embarrassed, she handed him her bag.

Dr. Martin walked back to his desk and put more ointment inside. He reached up and took a small transmitter off a shelf. He clicked it on, and immediately, a small red light flashed on his radar screen. Shaking his head, he dropped it into a side pocket of the bag and walked back out to Sabrina.

* * *

Barnaby, Gwen and Salem were on the dock near the Marine Research Institute, waiting for Sabrina.

"Hope you didn't mind sharing a room with Salem," said Gwen with a grin.

Salem snorted. "Of course no one's concerned that gill breath here kept me up half the night snoring."

Barnaby laughed. "No, we had a great time. I love Pay-Per-View!"

Salem pushed up his dark sunglasses. "Way to play it cool, merboy."

Sabrina came running down the dock with her bag. "I got it." She looked in the water and said, "Where's Spout?"

Barnaby shrugged. "Dolphins have the worst sense of time." He put two fingers in his mouth and let out an extremely loud whistle. Everyone cringed.

"I think I speak for everyone when I say, 'Ow!' " said Sabrina.

Squeak! Squeak! Spout had arrived and was playfully diving and splashing in the water below.

Sabrina was perched on Spout's back, her arms clinging to his neck. "Hang on," said Barnaby. "He'll get you there in no time."

"Dolphins," said Sabrina. "The only way to travel." Spout squeaked in agreement, flapped his tail with a flourish, and sped off over the water.

"I wish I had a dolphin to ride," said Gwen, still

standing on the dock. "It can't be too hard, can it? Sabrina always says it's just a matter of concentration." Gwen closed her eyes and clenched her fists. She peeked one eye open and then the other. Nothing happened.

"Frizzle!" she said, kicking the dock. *Why do all my spells backfire into something completely stupid, or just plain evaporate? Will my magic ever work?*

But something did happen. Salem had turned into a catfish! He flopped frantically on the deck, trying to get someone to notice him. No one did. With one last desperate leap for attention, he slid into the cold water below, completely unseen by Gwen or Barnaby.

Whoo-hoo! This is the most amazing ride of my life, thought Sabrina, holding onto Spout's smooth neck. *It's like we're gliding over the water, or flying . . . it's as magical as traveling through time or conjuring the best spell in the world.* Spout reared his tail, his signal that they were going underwater. She held her breath and stared, amazed, as they passed sea-carved coral formations and multicolored tropical fish. A giant clam opened its beautiful white shell in greeting. Soon, they passed through a curtain of luminous bubbles. The bubbles tickled and caressed her skin.

They surfaced in the middle of a gorgeous lagoon. It was the most beautiful place Sabrina had ever seen, at least on Earth. Floating nearby in the turquoise-blue water were several stunning mermaids. Their long, luminous hair flowed in the water, consumed by the ebbing tide. Their faces were sculpted perfection, and their eyes reflected the sea. On the algae-covered rocks rising out of the water was a mer-family. They were sunning themselves, sharing a family picnic on their favorite rock. When they saw Sabrina, they panicked and dove underwater.

"Wait!" she cried. "Don't go away. Barnaby sent me. I'm here to help you."

Dr. Martin was standing in front of the radar monitor at the Research Institute. A map of the island filled the screen, with a red light flashing on a small lagoon. His dark expression reflected off the glass as he shook his head in disbelief.

Chapter 8

Sabrina stood on the rocky edge of the small lagoon. The rocks were completely empty, and the calm, emerald sea was deserted. All of the mermaids had disappeared. Sabrina walked gingerly on the slippery rocks, wondering how she would ever get through to them. She grabbed her bag for reassurance and called out, "Barnaby sent me to help. I have medicine." She looked hopefully around. Not a mermaid in sight.

"You're not being very hospitable," she said irritably, flipping her wet hair. Finally, she knelt on a damp rock and cried, "Fin!" Her voice echoed in the lagoon, making it seem even emptier.

"We don't need your help," Fin said coldly. Sabrina spun around and saw Fin bobbing in the shallow water right next to her. Her tail, a stunning mixture of pinks, blues and greens, was covered with the same red patches that Barnaby had on his shoulder.

Instinctively, Sabrina reached out for her. "Fin. Your tail. You're sick. Let me . . ."

Fin whirled away, splashing Sabrina and her bag in the process. "I said we don't need you here. I'd rather die than have you perform any of your sorcery on me."

Sabrina swallowed hard. "Healing the sick is still done the old-fashioned way. No magic."

Fin shook her long, billowy hair, her lovely face frozen in fear. "Barnaby jeopardized the whole colony when he revealed himself to humans. Nothing will ever be the same."

"Is that so bad?" asked Sabrina quietly.

"We never got sick before humans showed up on our island," said Fin defensively.

Sabrina shook her head. "It's not the people on the island that are causing you to get sick. They're trying to put a stop to it right now." Sabrina leaned in as close to Fin as she could without getting splashed again. "Fin, I don't know how to make you understand, but I promise that nothing bad will happen to you, your brother or the colony. You have my word."

Fin swam a little bit closer. "Is Barnaby really okay?"

Sabrina smiled warmly. "He's great. His strength is back and his shoulder is almost completely

cleared up. He'll be home tomorrow." Sabrina un-
zipped her black, waterproof bag and took out some
ointment. "May I?" she asked Fin softly.

"Fine," Fin grumbled. "But, if I somehow end up
with legs, you're in a lot of trouble." Sabrina
laughed and put her hand over her heart. *Scout's
honor,* she thought to herself.

Fin pulled herself up onto the rock. Sabrina knelt
beside her and gently rubbed the ointment into her
tail.

Salem was not at all happy about being a catfish.
He had lost his fancy new sunglasses somewhere
between the dock and the huge wave that had nearly
knocked him out. *And besides,* he thought miserably, *fish are for eating, not being.* A group of red
snappers darted past and one of them lunged for his
tail. *"Ouch!"* he snarled, giving them his nastiest
fish-eye glare. He scurried past, and found a
carved-out crawl space in the coral.

He settled inside and moaned miserably. *Stoney
was right,* he thought to himself. *Gwen has the
worst concentration of any witch, and let's not even
mention her aim—*

Suddenly a long, silver barracuda peeked inside,
flashing rows of razor-sharp teeth. *Battle to the
death, it is,* thought Salem grimly, puffing out to his
largest gill and ready for action.

The barracuda eyed his opponent warily. He had
never seen a fish this ugly or less appetizing. Beady,

bulging, yellow eyes, and a miserable scowl confronted him. He spun around on his tail and fled to find a meal easier to digest.

Salem sighed and swam toward shore. *If I have to be somebody's dinner, I'd rather die in Hillary's mouth than a stranger's . . .*

BOOM! A cannon exploded over the rough seas. Amid the thunder of the shot, the Spellman sisters clutched each other, staring, dumbfounded, at the rising current of black powder swirling around them. "My goodness, where on Earth are we?" cried Hilda, coughing and sputtering beneath the mushrooming smoke.

The shot fell just short of the boat's side, crashing into the waves and forcing a rush of water to spray the deck.

"The question isn't so much where as when—I do believe we're passengers on an eighteenth-century ship," said Zelda, wiping her face.

Their ship groaned, rocking and shaking in the sea's angry grasp. The black cloud slowly evaporated, and behind it was the largest sailing ship they had ever encountered. It rose like a looming mountain out of the blue sea and sky, striking horror in their hearts.

Its flag fluttered softly in the wind; it was the stuff of nightmares, of terror in the dark. The skull and crossbones, the ancient symbol of the pirate flag. Instinctively, Hilda reached for her sister's hand.

"Well," said Zelda, her hands on her hips, "we may as well look the part if we're about to be boarded by pirates." She pointed, and they were transformed into high-born eighteenth-century women. Hilda's gown was a rich, dark blue that set off her eyes to perfection. Her bodice was made of velvet, with lace trimming. Zelda had conjured a lovely pink dress, with dark pink flowers embroidered on the bodice.

"Did you have to include the corset? That's really taking this a bit too far," said Hilda. But secretly, she was pleased with her dress—Zelda had picked perfectly.

"Fire!" the captain of their ship roared. Zelda looked down the deck—there were at least twelve cannons on each side—starboard to port. But she had a sinking feeling that they were outgunned.

The ship seemed to exhale deeply and gasp in pain as the shot went out. It tossed and tumbled on the sea. The pirate ship was so close, its figurehead seemed to be headed right at them! They screamed, watching as their ship's side was rammed. The deck groaned and trembled under them, sounding as if it were about to buckle up from beneath their feet.

A horrible screeching sound came next—the pirates had set their grappling hooks onto the ship and were rushing onto the deck!

"I know we really should be leaving . . ." said Hilda, her face flushed with excitement.

"Oh, yes," agreed Zelda, "but this is so fascinating, and we should at least make sure no one gets hurt . . ."

Swords were raised, and the unmistakable sound of metal against metal filled the air. The deck was suddenly packed with men—cursing, sweating, and crying out. But there was one man who had not yet boarded. And when he crossed over, a sudden hush followed.

"It's the Pirate King!" cried Zelda, clearly delighted with this new element. "He was the most feared man on the seven seas. He stole from the rich, and gave to the poor." They stared at him. He didn't look like a man who gave to the poor.

He towered above the fighting men on the deck below. His complexion was dark, his face mostly hidden in his wide-brimmed black hat. He wore a white shirt, open to his navel, revealing rows of hard muscle. His tan breeches clung to his legs, and his long black boots covered his knees.

Slowly, he made his way down onto the deck. He took off his hat, holding it in one hand, while the other brandished a long sword with a gilded handle. He scanned the deck with cold eyes and faced them like an executioner.

"Oh my," whispered Hilda. "Perhaps now's a good time to—"

The Pirate King was by their side in an instant. He made an exaggerated bow, his long, dark hair billowing in the sea breeze. Zelda was captivated. She had turned a deep red and was positively shaking. Hilda had never seen her like this before.

The Pirate King took Zelda's hand and kissed it. "Enchanted, fair lady," he said. "Now, please be so kind as to hand me all of your money and jewels."

Well, that will certainly burst her bubble, thought Hilda, relieved. Before Zelda could cry out in protest, Hilda pointed them right off the ship, leaving a very startled Pirate King and crew far behind . . .

The Marine Research Institute was buzzing with activity. Dr. Martin and his assistant were sitting at a table covered with maps and papers. The fax machines were spitting out hundreds of faxes, and the phones were ringing off the hook. The radar on the screen beeped menacingly over the lagoon.

"No one goes there," said his assistant, amazed. "That lagoon is completely inaccessible to boats."

"Well," observed Dr. Martin dryly, "*she* certainly didn't seem to have any problem. I'll find a way in. Call the Sydney Aquarium, make sure I can use one of their tanks. Just in case I find something, I want to be certain I have a place to keep it . . ."

Dr. Martin loved his reef. He knew everything there was to know about it—at least, he had thought that was true before Sabrina Spellman had arrived. On her first trip to the reef, she had spotted an extinct blue-spot butterfly fish. Beached dolphins were turning to her for help. And now, she had found her way to this lagoon. There was a secret there; he could feel it. A secret that would answer the question about those mermaid pictures. A secret that would explain young Miss Spellman's gift with the underwater world.

Sabrina had just finished rubbing the ointment into Fin's tail. She studied her handiwork carefully, satisfied. "There. All done. I'll leave the rest of this with you. Hopefully, I can find some more to send back with Barnaby."

"Thank you, Sabrina," said Fin sincerely. "I'm sorry I've been so difficult."

"It's all right. I'll be the first to admit, we're not the easiest species to get along with."

Fin gracefully slipped back into the water, her tail skipping over the surface like a wave of rainbows. She turned back to Sabrina. "Where are my manners? Would you like something to eat? You must be famished."

"Well," Sabrina admitted, "I am a little hun—"

Fin reached underwater and held up a living, breathing squid.

"—full from breakfast," she finished, beginning to feel ill.

"You sure?" asked Fin, biting the head off and chewing loudly. "They're delicious!"

Sabrina nodded, trying not to look as disgusted as she felt. "Never been so sure about anything in my life . . ."

* * *

As she returned to shore, Sabrina waved at Barnaby and Gwen, who were waiting up on the dock. Barnaby reached down and scooped her out of the water.

"You've been gone for hours," said Gwen. "We were beginning to be concerned."

"Once that Fin lets down her scales, she turns into a real talker," said Sabrina with a grin.

Barnaby looked worried. "She wasn't telling any stories, was she?"

"Maybe," Sabrina said playfully, turning to Gwen. "Let's just say Barnaby went through a very awkward phase."

Suddenly, Hillary leapt onto a nearby crate. "You're Salem's tormentors, right? Have you seen him lately?"

"No," said Sabrina. "I've been gone all day."

"He just kind of disappeared," said Gwen. "I thought he was spending the day with you."

"Well," said Hillary, licking a silky, white paw, "we have a confirmed dinner reservation, so I'm sure I'll see him then. Ta." Hillary jumped down and ran back toward the resort.

Sabrina, Gwen and Barnaby headed up the dock, gleefully imagining what Salem was up to. Stuffing himself at the all-you-can-eat breakfast buffet? Lapping up the heat in the sauna and hot tub? Reclining on a chaise longue drinking his second—no, third—fruit smoothie of the morning? Or, perhaps he had found the sushi chef of his dreams, and was on a plane to Tokyo at this very moment . . .

They walked past two fishermen who were dangling their lines in the water. Suddenly, one of them had a bite! The other one scooped it up with a net and they peered inside.

"She sure was right about the hot dog," said one of the fishermen.

"Yeah," said the other, looking at the fish's nasty expression. "But that's got to be the ugliest fish I've ever seen." Salem the Catfish spat a stream of water into his face. *Some vacation,* Salem the Catfish thought, rolling his puffy fish eyes.

At night, the lights of the restaurant cast a gentle glow on the boats in the marina. The maître d' walked through the crowded dining room, followed by a very regal Hillary. She was wearing a glittering jeweled collar, holding her graceful head up high against the stares and comments of the patrons. He led her to a private table overlooking the marina, and she leapt onto the soft, leather chair.

"Would you like to hear the specials?" he said out of habit. He looked down at her and sighed. "No, I don't suppose you do. Your owner already called in your order. I'll send your waiter right— Why am I even talking to you?"

"I was asking myself that same question," said Hillary, watching him walk off in a huff. "He's late and I didn't hear from him once today. More than curiosity is going to kill that cat if he stands me up," she said, licking her paws clean.

Sabrina, Gwen and Barnaby were seated at a far corner of the restaurant, looking over the menu.

"Unless we can figure out who and what is making you all sick and stop it, the ointment's not going to do much good," said Sabrina, reaching for a piece of bread.

"But," said Gwen, "you said that Dr. Martin thinks that the toxins are coming from illegal dumping."

Sabrina nodded. "But it could take months to catch whoever is doing it."

"We've talked about moving the colony, but we don't know where we'd go. We're very protected here. Or, we had been," said Barnaby.

Gwen turned to Sabrina. "Maybe you're right, Sabrina. I don't know if we can do this without Dr. Martin's help."

They looked through the crowded restaurant and saw Dr. Martin sitting alone at a table next to Hillary's. They shared the same breathtaking view of the marina. He had finished his dinner and was checking his bill.

A waiter came up to their table. "Good evening. If you'd like to follow me, you may select a fish from our tank and we'll prepare it to order." Sabrina, Gwen and Barnaby followed the waiter to the large fish tank in the center of the dining room.

Dr. Martin's assistant dashed into the restaurant and sat down at his table.

"We're all set," he said breathlessly. "Though I had to do a little fast talking when they asked what you needed the tank for."

Dr. Martin nodded and gave his bill to the waiter. "I've gone over all the charts and I think I've found a way into the lagoon. We'll have to dive, but we can still take nets, video equipment . . ."

His assistant looked around the crowded room nervously. "You sure we should be talking about this in here?"

"What?" said Dr. Martin, smiling wryly. "You afraid the cat's going to tell someone?"

The fur on the back of Hillary's collar bristled at the insult. "Like the cat gives a flying fig what you're talking about," she sniffed, watching them make their way to the door. "Men, I swear, they think the world revolves around them."

Sabrina, Gwen and Barnaby were still staring at the fish tanks. Bright red lobsters were packed into one tank, climbing all over each other. In the other, beautiful fish of all different shapes, colors and sizes darted around, swimming in circles.

"I feel kind of weird. What if these are some of the fish I met yesterday?" said Sabrina, peering into the tank.

Barnaby smiled broadly, and without the slightest hesitation, stuck his hand into the tank. He pulled

85

out a healthy, plump fish, and said with satisfaction, "This one." The waiter's eyebrows arched. "Excellent choice, sir. May I take that for you?"

"No, I'm fine," said Barnaby, seconds away from biting the fish's head off.

"Barnaby," Sabrina whispered, "give him the fish." Barnaby sighed and reluctantly handed it over. The waiter held the fish at arm's length, as it wiggled and flapped in his grasp.

Gwen was still staring at the tanks, trying to make up her mind. "Choices, choices," she said, reviewing her options as they swam by. She pressed her face against the glass for a closer inspection, when she came to face to face with Salem the Catfish! His beady yellow eyes blinked horribly into her much larger brown ones.

"Boo!" he said from inside the tank. "Aahh!" screamed Gwen, jumping back.

"Gwen, what's the matter?" asked Sabrina.

Gwen pointed and cried, "Look!"

Sabrina gasped in recognition and pointed, immediately turning Salem back into a cat. A very wet and pathetic cat, that is.

Salem hung over the side of the tank and moaned. "Couldn't you have gotten me out of the tank first?"

Someone in the restaurant pointed at the cat in the fish tank and let out a horrible shriek. Pandemonium ensued—plates were pushed away in disgust, and the waiters ran every which way to calm the patrons.

"I think I'll just have a salad," said Sabrina to a waiter passing by. Salem jumped down and shook himself off. Then, he dashed across the restaurant, over some very distraught diners, and leapt onto his chair with the great beach view.

Hillary was nowhere in sight. "I'm wet. I smell like fish. I've lost the woman of my dreams, and . . . she ate all the bread sticks."

Very, very early the next morning, Salem was hiking up through the brush, a camera swinging around his neck.

"It's not much farther," he said, turning back to Hillary, who was far behind. "Just stay on the path."

Hillary sidestepped a large mud puddle and shook her lovely white fur. "If you're trying to apologize for last night, getting me up before dawn to walk to the other side of the island isn't cutting it." If cats could pout, her lower lip would be a mile long.

Salem pushed through some thick undergrowth, and found himself standing on a high clearing overlooking the bay. "Ta da. We're here," he said.

The sunrise was truly magical. Bright pinks, oranges and yellows stretched as far as the horizon. Milky soft clouds floated, almost translucent above the clear, blue-green sea. Green parrots and cockatoos started to sing, welcoming the morning sky.

"One perfect sunrise," said Salem.

"Oh, Salem," purred Hillary, touching him gently with her paw. "It's glorious."

Salem strutted happily and pulled out his camera. "Okay, let's get a couple of shots for the folks back home. Say, 'Salem is super.' "

Hillary posed against the glorious sunrise as Salem clicked away. She frolicked by some wild-flowers, *Click!* lay on lush grass still covered with dew, *Click!* and smiled coquettishly at the camera. *Click! Make that a double Click!*

"How about I stick with 'cheese,' though Salem is pretty cute," she said. They leaned in for the first kiss of the new day, the sunrise glowing warmly behind them. Salem peeked one eye open, and saw a ship anchored not too far offshore . . .

Chapter 9

Sun spilled into the little bungalow by the beach. All of the clothes Sabrina had brought with her were laid out on the sea-blue bedspread. There were her favorite skintight cargo pants and brown velvet top, colorful T-shirts, and several miniskirts. Harvey's oversized football sweatshirt was curled up near her pillow. She glanced quickly at it and smiled. Something of his was with her, sharing this incredible experience. She finally decided on wearing her denim cut-offs and a light blue tank top. Gwen was wearing a black U2 T-shirt and baggy khaki shorts. She was applying a generous amount of mousse to her cropped hair, which was sticking up every which way.

After much pressing and brushing, Gwen gazed into the mirror framed with seashells, satisfied. She plopped down onto her bed, pushing aside wet towels from this morning's bath and piles of candy wrappers and magazines.

"Barnaby turns back into a merman today," said Gwen thoughtfully. "You going to be okay with that?"

Sabrina nodded, rubbing suntan lotion on her legs. "Yeah. I just wish there was more we could do."

"What?" asked Gwen.

"I decided I'm going to talk to Dr. Martin. He's a scientist, right? He'll be rational." Sabrina picked up her waterproof bag, searching inside. "I at least have to ask him for some more ointment. I promised Fin that I'd . . ." She stopped suddenly as she pulled the little tracking device out of the side pocket.

"What's that?" asked Gwen, leaning over.

"I don't know," said Sabrina, peering at the little black box with a flashing red light. "I think it's a tracking device. The kind they tag whales with so they can be followed."

Sabrina and Gwen looked at each other in silence. "You don't think he put that in your bag on purpose, do you?" asked Gwen.

"It's the only way it could have gotten there," said Sabrina quietly.

"Then," said Gwen, watching the red light flash like a heartbeat, "he knows where the colony is . . ."

Sabrina grabbed Gwen's arm. "Find Barnaby. Now I definitely have to talk to Dr. Martin."

* * *

On the way down the beach to the Marine Research Institute, Sabrina's thoughts were clouded with confusion. *How could Dr. Martin have done this to me? I promised Fin that no harm would come to her or her colony—what have I done?* Sabrina took a deep breath and willed herself to calm down. *This was major bad news—I guess I was right not to trust Dr. Martin in the beginning . . . but if I had told him the truth at first, maybe none of this would have happened . . .*

Sabrina marched past the gate and pushed through the door. The only sounds were the computer's humming and the ticking of a large metal clock high up on the wall. Sabrina brushed past the tanks full of fish, and tables strewn with charts and papers. She rushed over to Dr. Martin's desk, her heart pounding a mile a minute.

"Hello? Dr. Martin?" No one was there. *Oh, no!* thought Sabrina, beginning to panic. *Has he already set off for the mermaid lagoon? Am I too late?* She ran out of the building as quickly as she could.

Salem and Hillary were sitting at a picnic table on a small, charming patch off the resort's main pathway. Large, flowering trees circled them, bathing them in their fragrance. The pictures they had taken that morning were spread out on the picnic table. They were perfectly awful. In one, Hillary's head was chopped off. In the second, she was horribly out of focus. In the others, he managed to catch a piece of her tail and a lovely shot of her ear but the rest of her body was nowhere to be seen.

Salem sighed. "I don't know about you, but I think they're kind of arty." Hillary rolled her eyes.

Sabrina was running down the path when she spotted them through the trees.

"Has either of you seen Dr. Martin?" she asked. She looked down at the photographs and grinned. "Wow, these pictures are almost as bad as pictures you took for last year's Christmas card. Nothing but knees."

Salem gave her his whatever-do-you-mean-I'm-an-artist look. No one bought it. Enjoying Salem's well-deserved put-down, Hillary decided to be helpful. "I heard your doctor friend talk about storming some lagoon this morning. He was quite full of himself."

"Oh, no, I hope I'm not too late," said Sabrina, about to run off. But something in one of the pictures caught her eye. "Can I take this? Thanks. Gotta go." She jogged down the path and disappeared around the corner.

"Is she always like this?" asked Hillary.

Salem let out a deep sigh. His yellow eyes filled with emotion, trying to express how difficult life was as her familiar. "Pretty much."

Hillary didn't buy that one either.

Dr. Martin's boat, *The Sea Wasp*, was almost ready to take off. His assistants were piling in diving gear, video equipment, and huge nets. Nets big enough to catch a dolphin. A whale. Or even a mermaid colony . . .

Sabrina was running down the dock, shouting, "Dr. Martin!"

He turned around and waved good-naturedly. "Sabrina, good morning. We're just heading out to try to verify your *Chaetodon plebeius* sighting. I'll let you know if we have any luck." He got back on the boat, signaling that the conversation was over.

I don't think so, thought Sabrina. "You're not going out to look for my fish," she stated coldly, taking out the tracking device. "Unless you think it's hiding out in a lagoon on the other side of the island."

Dr. Martin and his assistants stared at her, dumbfounded. "Seems you're always one step ahead of me, Sabrina."

Sabrina pointed at the device. "Why would you do this?" Her eyes were sad, and she seemed to Dr. Martin like a lost little girl.

Dr. Martin stepped back onto the dock. "You weren't honest with me," he said gently. "I wasn't with you. Sorry, but you made the rules."

Sabrina squared her shoulders and looked him straight in the eye. "This isn't a game. You can't go there. Please. You don't know what you're doing."

"I know more about this reef than you could ever hope to know," he said curtly, facing Sabrina, the capable young woman, once more. "If there's something out there, I'm going to find it." He took the tracking device out of her hand. "And thanks to you, I know the first place I'm going to look." He turned and got back on the boat.

"I'm not going to let you do this," said Sabrina angrily.

Dr. Martin shot her a cold stare. "I'd like to see you try and stop me." The boat began to pull away from the dock. Dr. Martin was still looking at her, his expression a mixture of respect and anger.

Sabrina held out her finger. "Watch me," she whispered defiantly.

Chapter 10

Sabrina was standing on the dock near the Marine Research Institute, watching Dr. Martin's boat, *The Sea Wasp*, sail away from the bay. He was heading out for the mermaid colony, and once he found it, their lives would be changed forever. He had huge nets on that boat—nets that would be used to capture the mermaids and take them back here. For research. Sabrina closed her eyes, trying desperately not to imagine Fin's cries of terror at being trapped in a net like bait, and hauled off by people staring at her like she was a freak. The ape-woman at the circus. The tattooed fat lady. *Her fears of humans are now grounded,* thought Sabrina miserably. *What have I done?*

She turned to look toward shore and saw Barnaby and Gwen running up the dock at breakneck speed.

95

"Sabrina, is it true?" asked Barnaby, pain shooting through his handsome features. "Does he know where the colony is?"

"Yes, he knows, but . . ." said Sabrina dully. *I don't know what to say to him . . . He trusted me. They all trusted me. There must be something I can do. . . .*

Barnaby paced the dock, his hands clenching into fists. "What are you just standing around here for? You have to do something. I can't even swim there to try and warn them." He walked to the end of the dock, looking far into the horizon. "Please, change me back. I don't want to be a man."

Sabrina went to Barnaby's side and put her arm around his shoulder. "There's less than an hour before the spell reverses itself. You've got to calm down." She rubbed his arms encouragingly and looked up at him. "We're not going to let anything happen to the colony." Her face was firm and proud. But inside, her stomach was doing cartwheels.

"I say we zap a tsunami," said Gwen. "Or maybe a giant squid." Sabrina gave her a give-me-a-break look. Gwen shrugged. "I'm just brainstorming."

The Sea Wasp had moved so far toward the horizon, it was just a white speck on the distant water. Soon, it disappeared completely.

"I can't even see the boat anymore," said Barnaby sadly. He looked back toward land and noticed Lookout Point, where he and Sabrina had gone hiking. "Maybe I can see them from the Point." He ran quickly down the dock.

"Barnaby! Wait!" cried Sabrina.

"He's really starting to get the hang of those legs," observed Gwen with a smirk. Gwen looked up at the clear sky. Bright rays from the sun were flickering across the calm sea.

"I wish we could conjure up a huge storm. That would keep them away from the lagoon."

Sabrina stopped and clasped Gwen's hands. "Gwen, that's a great idea!"

"Really?" said Gwen, surprised.

"Yeah. It's perfect. Come on. I've wanted to try this spell ever since I got my license," said Sabrina. They hurried down the dock toward the water's edge.

Salem was lying with his head on Hillary's lap, enjoying the view of the harbor from the top of Lookout Point. A beautifully arranged fruit and cheese plate was within easy reach, as were delicious spreads, patés, caviar, and shrimp cocktail. They were surrounded by picnic baskets overflowing with mouth-watering sandwiches, corn on the cob, and freshly baked cookies.

"Now this is what I call heaven," said Salem, grabbing a piece of fried chicken from a bucket beside them. "You, me, alone with eleven picnic baskets and no . . ."

Out of the corner of his eye, he noticed Barnaby running up the path to the top of the hill.

". . . distractions," finished Hillary, watching Barnaby disappear behind some trees.

"Pay no attention to Fish Boy. More paté?" said Salem, offering her a crackerful.

Hillary purred and ate the cracker out of his paw, smiling happily.

Woosh! A bolt of the coldest wind Zelda had ever felt whipped past her with incredible intensity. She raised her hand over her eyes to shield them from the bright glare, and could not believe what she saw.

Mounds of snow and ice spread out for what seemed like forever, and the sun beat down mercilessly on the vast expanse of whiteness, but offered little warmth.

"The Arctic Circle? The North Pole? Somewhere in Alaska on top of a glacier?" gasped Zelda. She was so cold, it took several moments for her fingers to uncurl and point them into heavy down coats, boots, mittens and scarves.

"There must be a reason for this . . . what was I thinking of? Oh yes, something about getting as far away from that ship and the eighteenth century as possible. And definitely the ocean. I'm sure I mentioned that," said Hilda, gazing at a snowy slope that led to the frozen sea.

"Well, I don't think we have to worry about bumping into any kangaroos or gum trees at the moment. I'm really starting to wonder about your sense of geography, Hilda. Australia is in another hemisphere entirely," said Zelda, stomping off into the snow.

They walked along the snow covered ice, their furry boots squishing and squeaking, leaving two pairs of footprints in the clear white expanse.

"Look up!" cried Hilda, pointing to a ragged snow-covered cliff that hung over the ice.

"Let me guess," said Zelda dryly. "A palm tree? A forest of eucalyptus trees full of furry koala bears?"

Not a koala bear in sight; instead, thousands of icicles, some maybe twenty feet long, hung from the top of the cliff. The sun's tremendous glare flickered and glowed off them, creating a stream of rainbow-colored light that danced on the white snow and over the icy sea.

"This," said Zelda, with a sharp intake of breath, "is worth the mix-up. I don't remember the last time I saw anything so dazzling."

The sisters ran over the packed snow, slipping and falling along the way, toward the frozen sea. They stopped near a hole in the ice and peered inside, into the dark, inconceivably freezing water that swirled below.

Suddenly, there was a ripple in the hole and the top half of a seal popped up to greet them.

Hilda clapped her hands, delighted. "I thought I was thinking about dolphins when I was conjuring, but . . ."

"Well," said Zelda, leaning close to the seal who

eyed her with a soft, curious stare, "a seal really isn't so off the mark. I mean, they are mammals that live underwater."

Hilda smiled. "Oh, Sabrina would love this! Do you think we could pet it?"

Zelda shrugged. "Well, we can try . . ." They bent down near the hole, and reached out to touch the seal's soft, black skin. The seal pulled away at first, frightened, but eventually he let them scratch behind his ears.

"Sabrina's not the only one who'd be in heaven right now," said Zelda. "Can you imagine Salem's delight at being so close to such a large sea creature?"

"He'd be licking his lips and drooling everywhere—and in this climate, it would freeze his whiskers off," said Hilda with a grin.

Suddenly, they heard loud cracking and crumbling noises. "Uh-oh," squealed Hilda. The ice around the hole was falling into the frozen sea.

"What the—" Zelda gasped, feeling something large and formidable moving under her in the water. A huge gray head, armed with fourteen-foot tusks, burst through the snow-covered ice next to the seal's breathing hole.

"Why, it's a walrus!" exclaimed Hilda, too stunned to be scared. The walrus began to groan and started shifting his heavy bulk onto the surface of the ice. *Crack!* A piece of ice perilously close to Hilda's foot started to shift under the incredible weight.

The sisters screamed and ran off the ice. They

stopped, catching their breath, and looked back toward the water. Something was standing farther out on the ice that hadn't been there before. Zelda looked up and blinked. Across the frozen water, standing white against the enveloping whiteness, stood a magnificent polar bear. "Uh . . . Hilda," said Zelda, her throat tightening with fear and wonder. "We're not the only things attracted to seals. . . ."

Hilda's jaw dropped. "Oh boy—we better get out of here!" They grabbed each other's hand and started to run away. The problem was, the polar bear decided to chase them.

"Why couldn't we have dropped into Santa's house for some warm milk and cookies?" cried Hilda, struggling to keep up. "Shared a ride on a reindeer? Warmed our hands on an open fire—"

"Grrrr!"

Twenty yards behind them stood a very irritated and very large polar bear. "He does look hungry, doesn't he," said Hilda, clutching the puffy sleeve of Zelda's coat.

"I think I've had enough of this winter wonderland," said Zelda, raising her finger. In moments, they were gone. The polar bear fell backward, startled by their sudden disappearance. He lumbered over to their footprints and, after a long sniff, lay down in the cold snow.

Sabrina and Gwen were on the beach, staring far out at the horizon. "Sabrina, are you sure about this? Weather spells can be very dangerous."

"Of course I'm sure. Well, pretty sure." Sabrina smiled confidently at her friend. "I can give it a try, can't I?"

"Be careful," said Gwen nervously.

Sabrina stepped into the water. The waves lapped at her feet, the current pulling her deeper. She waded out until the water reached her bellybutton and took a deep breath.

Focus! she thought to herself. *This is for a very good cause.* She pointed her finger toward the distant sky and started her incantation:

"Waves to toss with violent motion / A squall upon the tranquil ocean / Clouds and rain. Thunder and lightning / Give me a storm that's truly frightening." She took a step back in the water and blew as hard as she could. Immediately, the wind started howling and blowing over the sea. Ominous black clouds darkened what had been a beautiful sunny day. A storm had come to Hamilton Island.

"Wicked!" cried Gwen from the shore. "Sabrina, you did it!"

Dr. Martin and his assistant were standing on the deck of *The Sea Wasp*. The sky had suddenly turned black, and the wind was whipping the boat around the high waves as if the huge yacht was a child's toy.

"Where did that come from?" Dr. Martin exclaimed, furious.

"We can't take this kind of weather. We have to turn around," his assistant pointed out gravely.

Dr. Martin looked out at the rising waves and the threatening skies. Angrily, he pounded his fist against the wheel. *I will reach this mysterious lagoon,* he thought. *The weather won't be able to keep me from it forever, and I will uncover what mysteries lie there . . .*

Barnaby was staring down at the beach from the very top of Lookout Point. He saw the dark clouds roll in over the bay and felt the wind stirring up. "Look!" he cried. "Sabrina created a huge storm." He shaded his hand over his eyes and could just barely make out *The Sea Wasp* heading back to shore. "Yes!" he shouted happily. "They're turning around."

Salem, Hillary and their eleven picnic baskets were seated nearby. Salem was determined to ignore not only Fish Boy's comments but also his presence at their picnic.

"So," he said to Hillary, "read any good books lately?"

Sabrina and Gwen were looking up at the black sky. Sabrina smiled, relief flooding over her. "See," she called to Gwen, "nothing to it. I don't know what you were so worried . . ."

Suddenly, the sky exploded in a huge flash. A glowing bolt of lightning hit the water, just missing

Sabrina. The force of the impact threw her up out of the water and onto the beach.

"Sabrina!" cried Gwen, running up to her. Gwen knelt beside her, stroking her hair. Sabrina did not respond. She was unconscious.

Barnaby was dancing and laughing out loud. "You did it!" he cried, gesturing to Gwen and Sabrina at the water's edge. "They're coming back!" Barnaby looked closer at the beach and realized that Sabrina was lying on the sand, not moving. Gwen motioned frantically for him to help.

"Salem, something's wrong with Sabrina," said Barnaby, feeling a horrible tightness in his throat.

Salem yanked a bunch of grapes away from Hillary's eager mouth. "What's the matter?"

"I think she's hurt."

Salem looked around and saw a pick-up truck near the path. Several hikers were walking away from it and toward a path in the woods.

"Follow me!" said Salem. He glanced down at Hillary, who was surrounded by piles of food. "I'm sorry, but . . ." he began awkwardly.

Hillary, plopping a juicy grape into her mouth, said, "Just go already."

"I love you," said Salem, smiling into Hillary's inscrutable eyes.

Hillary almost choked on the juicy grape. "What did he say?" she sputtered, watching Salem and Barnaby run off toward the truck. She sighed and lay back down on the soft blanket, dreamily contemplating picnic baskets stuffed with mouth-watering treats, and a handsome black cat who had remarkably good taste.

The sky had turned a threatening blue-black color and lightning blazed around them like it was the Fourth of July. Gwen shook Sabrina gently. She didn't move. Gwen closed her eyes and whispered, "Oh, please. Just this once." She curled her hand into a fist and they disappeared off the beach, leaving only the imprints of their bodies in the sand.

Moments later, they appeared in their bungalow. Sabrina was lying on the bed, her damp blond hair spread over the sea-blue bedspread. Gwen was sitting by her side, her eyes squeezed shut. Slowly, she opened her eyes and smiled. "Oh, thank goodness, we're not in Greenland." *Finally! When I needed it most my spell worked . . .*

Barnaby was sitting behind the wheel of the truck, with Salem right beside him. "Go!" Barnaby ordered the truck. Nothing happened. "What's the matter with this animal?" he asked Salem. "It's lazier than a sea cow."

Salem shook his head. "Turn it on," he said dryly.

Barnaby stared at him, obviously not comprehending.

"The key. Turn the key, baithead!" Barnaby

turned the key and the truck roared. It sounded as if it had just woken up from a bad dream, and was none too happy about it.

"Just pull that thing back," said Salem, gesturing to the emergency brake. "And push down on the pedal to your . . ."

The truck had already started rolling down the hill. "Scratch that! Turn the wheel!" commanded Salem, as they narrowly escaped driving off the road and straight into a tree.

In the bungalow, Gwen was flipping through the magic book while Sabrina was lying unconscious on the bed. *Hmm . . . Saving spells, German recipe for sauerkraut, star gazing—not to be confused with star riding, see section on how to get around the universe with no money . . . Here we go, storm raising . . . Gosh, this is a major bummer of a spell. . . .*

Gwen looked up when Sabrina suddenly stirred.

"What happened? Where am I?" she asked, trying to sit up. Thinking the better of it, she collapsed back down.

"We're back in the room," said Gwen. "You blasted yourself right out of the ocean. But you're going to be okay. You just need to rest."

Sabrina sighed. "But it worked."

Gwen nodded slowly. "Yeah, but . . ." She pointed at the magic book. "That spell has three pages of warnings attached to it. The first of which is don't stand in the water!"

"Oh," said Sabrina. "I knew I was forgetting something. My neck is killing me."

"That should pass, but the electric charge is going to interfere with your magic for a couple of hours."

"Well, hopefully, if the storm worked, I won't need it for a while," said Sabrina, looking out the glass doors at the raging sky. Clouds were sweeping in from the bay, forcing the waves higher and casting a dark shadow over the island.

The pick-up truck careened violently from side to side, nearly throwing Salem out the window or into the dashboard with every wild turn. Barnaby was madly swinging the wheel back and forth, unaware that this was a one-lane road.

"Just my luck," moaned Salem, his nails digging into the seat. "I meet the woman of my dreams and I die in a fiery wreck." His yellow eyes widened in terror. "Watch out!" he cried. Barnaby hit the brakes and spun the wheel, narrowly missing an oncoming car.

A crew member tied *The Sea Wasp* to the end of the dock, as Dr. Martin and his assistant jumped off the boat.

"Hurry up," said Dr. Martin. "We have to secure the Institute before the storm hits." His assistant stopped and pointed to the clearing skies over the ocean. The dark clouds were receding rapidly as rays of golden sunlight played upon the water's surface. The storm was evaporating before their eyes.

Sabrina was sitting up in bed, rubbing her neck. Gwen handed her a cup of tea and sat by her side.

"Thanks," said Sabrina. "I'm already starting to feel a little . . ." She looked over at the little clock on the table. "Is that the time?"

Sabrina and Gwen looked at each other and shouted in unison, "Barnaby!"

The pick-up truck had miraculously made its way down Lookout Point and was speeding past the center of town, heading for the dock. Barnaby seemed to have things a bit more under control, and had finally figured out the difference between the gas pedal and the brake.

"I knew I could tame this beast," said Barnaby proudly. Suddenly, his legs began to glow. Light flickered and swirled around them. He looked at Salem desperately.

"Uh-oh," said Salem weakly. The forty-eight hours were up. Barnaby's human legs were magically transformed back into a tail. The huge tail unfolded, taking up most of the cabin, and nearly crushing Salem under its weight.

"Get your smelly flipper out of my—" Salem glanced out the window. "Look out!" he screamed. Barnaby screamed along with him, desperately trying to steer and work the pedals with his tail.

They were headed straight for Dr. Martin, who was walking up to the gates in front of the Marine Research Institute. He did not see the pick-up truck barreling toward him at full speed.

Barnaby flapped his tail helplessly against the pedals. The animal wasn't stopping. Salem had his paws over his eyes, screaming in terror. Dr. Martin finally looked up and saw the truck hurtling toward him. He managed to dive out of the way as Barnaby spun the wheel and the truck skidded to a stop, seconds before crashing into the gates.

Salem looked through his paws. *Am I alive? Thank God. I'm going to get Fish Boy for this . . .*

Dr. Martin ran over to the driver's side of the truck and yanked the door open furiously. Barnaby and his glorious tail flopped onto the ground in front of him. "Hey, Doc, shoulder's really doing a lot better . . ."

Dr. Martin stared at Barnaby, his expression a mixture of shock, delight and anger.

Chapter 11

The dock was swarming with tourists, creating a colorful sea of bright bathing suits, towels, shorts and sundresses moving under the glowing sun. People were running around with their cameras, talking animatedly, and pointing at the water. Some started running toward the resort, dashing past Sabrina and Gwen, who were standing by the dock's entrance. They looked at each other, surprised. "What's happening?" Gwen asked, amazed by the crowd.

"Where's everyone going?" she asked a passerby. He continued on, caught up in the mad dash toward the resort.

Sabrina pushed past the people and ran along the deck, scanning the water. "Barnaby," she called out to the clear sea below. Above, the dark clouds had disappeared, and the sun shined its warmth on the rolling waves. Gwen ran up to her, breathless.

"Where is he?" asked Sabrina. "He knows this is the first place we'd look for him." Gwen pointed to the end of the dock where Dr. Martin's yacht was tied up.

"The Sea Wasp is back. At least we won't have to worry about Dr. Martin for a while," said Gwen. She pushed some unruly strands of chestnut-brown hair out of her eyes, relieved.

"Think again," a familiar voice said from behind a storage locker. Salem leapt on top of the large box and faced them.

"Salem, what happened?" asked Sabrina, reaching over to pet his bristling black fur.

Salem sighed dramatically. "Oh, Sabrina, it was awful. I may never ride in a car again . . ."

Sabrina glared at him. "I meant, to Barnaby."

"Oh . . ." Salem picked up a paw and began to clean it. After several long and intense licks, he said with a bored drawl, "Martin captured him and has him locked up in the resort's swimming pool."

Sabrina and Gwen gasped and exchanged a fearful look. "We've got to get him out," said Sabrina, staring out into the deep sea.

Suddenly, a beautiful tail, glowing with shiny scales, fluttered in the water. Fin's long hair cascaded down her swan-like neck, and floated like a soft blond pillow behind her.

"Sabrina, is it true?" she demanded. "Have they

captured Barnaby? I was worried that he hadn't come back."

Sabrina nodded her head sadly. "Yes, it's true." Her throat constricted and she fought to hold back tears. "But . . ."

Fin's lovely face hardened in anger. "You promised nothing would happen to him . . . to us. You gave me your word."

The unmistakable groan of a large helicopter overhead forced them all to look up. It was flying low over the sea, on its way to the helipad to land.

"Sabrina," cried Gwen, pointing up. "I think it's a news helicopter."

Salem, who had finished grooming one paw and had moved on to the other one, smiled smugly. "I'm going to be on television."

Sabrina and Fin gazed quietly at the helicopter and then back to each other. "Fin, I'm sorry," said Sabrina softly. *How in the world am I going to fix this mess without my magic?*

"Barnaby was a fool to have trusted you. Let's hope I can save the rest of us." Fin swam a few yards back and dove under an oncoming wave, disappearing into the blue sea.

The pool area had been cleared of guests, but an excited crowd surrounded the pool gates, trying to get a look inside. A *Sea Wasp* crew member was standing by the gate, trying to keep the area closed to the public. "What is it—is it a merman?" people asked. He guarded the gate in silence, his eyes giving nothing away.

Barnaby was alone in the resort's swimming pool. He circled the pool and flipped onto his back, gazing at a curious crew member who was standing near the diving board. Barnaby raised his magnificent tail and let it fall hard into the water near the diving board.

Splash!

Dr. Martin walked onto the pool deck from the resort lobby. "How's he doing?" he asked a crew member. Barnaby waved at Dr. Martin with his tail and headed back underwater.

"Fine," the crewman said, sopping wet. "He's got a delightful sense of humor." Dr. Martin smiled wryly and turned as his assistant came up behind him.

"I've made the arrangements," the assistant said, reviewing his clipboard. "The transportation to Sydney is on its way. And CNN just landed."

"What?" cried Dr. Martin angrily. He dashed back into the lobby, pushing past the huge potted palm trees and hordes of eager tourists trying to steal a view of the pool. He spotted the manager talking to a group of reporters and cameramen.

He brushed past the reporters, and stood face to face with the manager. "Who told you to call the press?" he demanded, grabbing his arm. "This is my show."

The manager shook off his hand and said in a huff, "And it's my pool." He paused, and looked at

Dr. Martin thoughtfully. "If you really have a mer-thing in there, then this resort is definitely sharing the prize." He turned back to the reporters, signaling that their conversation was over. Dr. Martin stared at him, dumbfounded, and brushed his hand through his hair. *What kind of sideshow have I created?* he thought sadly. *This is my reef. My little part of the ocean. I have spent my life protecting it. And now this . . .*

Gwen and Sabrina, with Salem curled up in her arms, ran into the crowded lobby. "We'll never be able to get him out through this crowd," said Gwen, looking nervously at the jammed room.

"Maybe we can go through the other side," suggested Sabrina. She looked down at Salem and said, "Try to get to him and make sure he's all right."

"You can count on—" Salem's eyes widened. Nearby, the resort staff had laid out a table of food and refreshments for the curious onlookers. "Look, macadamia nuts!"

Sabrina placed him on the floor and said sternly, "Go!"

He weaved his way though the throngs of people and disappeared through the door that led to the pool. Satisfied, Sabrina and Gwen turned to leave and tried to get past the swelling crowd. Suddenly, a familiar smile walked past, with locks of sun-kissed hair and snorkeling equipment. Gwen blushed and stopped walking.

"G'day, Gwen," said Jerome, flashing his knock-out smile. "Been looking all over for you."

Sabrina looked at her watch impatiently. "Gwen, remember, we're kind of in a hurry . . ." Then, she saw Dr. Martin talking to a reporter near the entrance to the pool. "I'll be right back," she called over her shoulder. She narrowed her eyes, squared her shoulders, and charged across the room.

A reporter was busy writing on his notepad, listening to Dr. Martin eagerly.

"I'm not going to confirm or deny anything," Dr. Martin began, "until we can properly analyze our discovery and . . ." He looked up and spotted Sabrina rushing toward him. "Excuse me a moment," he said, distracted. He and Sabrina met halfway through the packed lobby. "Sabrina, I suppose I have you to thank and blame for all of this."

Her eyes flared and she said quietly, "Who's the poacher now, Dr. Martin?" Without waiting for a reply, Sabrina turned on her heels and marched back to Gwen.

Dr. Martin shook his head and walked back to the reporter, facing him with an uneasy smile.

Sabrina tapped Gwen on the shoulder. "Okay, we better get out of here." Gwen gazed into Jerome's warm eyes. "Sabrina, Jerome was just telling me the funniest—" She paused for a moment, taking in

Sabrina's annoyed expression. "I've got to go," Gwen said quickly to Jerome.

They started to push toward the door, when Sabrina stopped suddenly. She spun around and gave Jerome a long, hard stare. Gwen, momentarily startled, looked at Sabrina looking at Jerome. Slowly, a smile formed on her lips and extended all the way to her ears. They nodded at each other, grinning.

"What are you sheilas lookin' at me so funny for?" asked Jerome defensively. They each grabbed one very tan and very strong arm, and pulled him toward the door.

Salem strutted by the pool and watched Barnaby swim in circles at the bottom. *How do I get Fish Boy's attention? What I really need is some soy sauce and sticky rice . . .* thought Salem, leaning in to the pool and licking his lips greedily.

An extremely large and scaly tail hit the surface, startling Salem out of his sushi fantasy and dousing him with a stream of water. Barnaby popped his head up and smiled.

"Salem, finally. Where's Sabrina? Is she all right?"

Salem stepped gingerly out of a puddle. "She's fine, but her magic is a little out of whack."

Barnaby placed his arms on the side of the pool, and looked up at Salem imploringly. "She's going to get me out of here, isn't she?"

Salem sighed. "Ah, sure. Just keep telling yourself that." He looked up and saw Hillary darting through the pool gate.

"Hillary!" cried Salem, delighted. Hillary smiled, her lovely white tail flicking suggestively behind her. "I figure, why keep fighting it. Is there anything I can do?" Salem gazed into her mesmerizing gray eyes, looking away reluctantly when he saw a *Sea Wasp* crew member rushing over.

"Hey, you cats!" he cried. "Get away from there!"

"Find Sabrina," said Salem quickly. "Tell her five minutes. North Gate. I'll distract the guard."

Hillary leapt onto the diving board, and turned back to Salem. "I think I love you, too." Then, she gracefully jumped onto the wet tiles and disappeared through the lobby door.

Salem stared after her, flabbergasted. "What did she say?"

Sabrina was in Salem's deluxe suite, nervously looking around. The place was, of course, a complete disaster area. The empty room-service trays had mysteriously multiplied in number since her last visit, and jars of half-eaten nuts, candy bar wrappers and newspapers littered the floor. She sighed and reached for one of the carts, stacked with last night's leftovers. She wheeled it out of the room, and was just closing the door behind her when Hillary sprung onto the cart.

"Hello, Sabrina. Hillary. I don't think we've ever

really been properly introduced." She settled down between the silver bread tray, a half-full porcelain coffee cup, and the salt and pepper shakers.

"Charmed," said Sabrina. "Don't mean to be rude, but I'm kind of in the middle of a crisis."

Hillary leaned in close. "Salem said he'll distract the guard. You should be able to get in on the north end of the pool."

Sabrina smiled, relief warming her face. "Great. Let's go." Hillary's claws dug into the white table-cloth as Sabrina pushed the cart down the hall at record speed.

The lobby was full to capacity. Hordes of people were crowded against desks, chairs, and tables, pressing to get closer to the opening by the pool. The manager was standing by the door, sweating furiously as he gazed at the excited mob of tourists.

"Tell the governor that we can't wait any longer," he told a staff member by his side. The manager took a deep breath and mopped his brow with his handkerchief.

"All right," he said to the assembled group, "if everyone is ready . . ."

Dr. Martin pushed his way through the people, stumbling over plants and table legs as he rushed past. "I told you, it's a matter of significant scientific importance," he said to the manager angrily. "You can't go out there."

The manager eyed him warily. "I'd like to see

you try to stop me." He turned and, with much pomp and ceremony, opened the doors to the pool. People spilled outside, almost trampling each other in their rush to look inside the pool. The manager stood by the diving board, surrounded by hordes of shocked onlookers. His face fell, and his shoulders sagged with humiliation. "Is this your idea of a joke?" he demanded. Dr. Martin looked up, bewildered. Then, he gazed at the pool, and his head began to pound.

Jerome was lying by the pool decked to the nines in his mermaid regalia. His plastic sequined tail flopped against the tiles as he strummed his ukulele. He grinned his million-dollar smile and waved warmly to the silent crowd.

"Sabrina," murmured Dr. Martin, clutching his throbbing head. "Wait here, we'll be right back," he said to the manager as he and his assistant headed for the door.

"Where are you going?" sputtered the manager, watching them leave. "You can't do this . . ."

Unfazed by the perplexed stares from the crowd, Jerome launched into a rousing version of "My Bonnie Lies Over the Ocean."

> *"My bonnie lies over the ocean,*
> *My bonnie lies over the sea . . ."*

☆

Chapter 12

☆

Sabrina and Gwen were pushing the room-service cart, with Barnaby sprawled out on top, through the resort's open-air lobby. His large fish tail hung over the end, flapping furiously as they charged down the hall, through the doors and onto the outdoor pathway.

They struggled through the gravel walkway, and pushed forward toward the dock, frantically looking behind them as they ran in the hot midday sun.

Dr. Martin dashed out of the lobby with *The Sea Wasp* crew right behind him. "There's only one place they could be heading," he said, looking toward the beach. "The dock." Without a word, they ran along the shore, heading toward the dock with rigid determination.

Sabrina and Gwen tried with all their might to push the cart up a steep incline on the resort's beachside path. One of the wheels slammed against a large boulder, and Barnaby's tail flew up into the air, as he grabbed onto the metal sides. Sabrina wiped sweat off her face, and was about to kick the offending rock out of the way, when Barnaby's large fish tail came down with a swift blow, and knocked it onto the grass.

They pushed the cart as hard as they could, and finally reached the top of the hill. They caught their breath for a moment, and rushed forward, careening wildly around a sudden bend in the path. "Hold on," Sabrina cried, as the cart flew past the corner. Barnaby managed to hold on and sail past, but Sabrina and Gwen stumbled and the cart flew out of their hands.

The cart hurtled down, with Barnaby clinging on for dear life. Sabrina and Gwen raced after it, screaming "Hold on!"

The merman glided down the beachside path on the room-service cart, zooming past an elderly couple sitting on a bench. The couple had a front row seat to see the sparkling fish tail rolling by. They looked at each other, shrugged, and returned to their reading.

Sabrina made a desperate leap for the cart's handle and grabbed on, using her feet as brakes to control it.

"Sabrina, look out!" cried Gwen, pointing up the path. Several of Dr. Martin's crew were running toward her, their arms outstretched and ready to grab Barnaby in an instant.

Sabrina swerved the cart onto another pathway, and sprinted toward the dock. It took her a few moments to push the cart up onto the wooden dock, and once she did, it was clear sailing ahead. She ran halfway down the dock, and quickly looked behind her. Dr. Martin's crew were gaining on her. In desperation, she gave the cart one final push. It hurtled toward the end of the dock and smacked into a wooden post. Barnaby flew into the air, his tail making a graceful arc against the sky, and then he dove into the clear water below.

Sabrina let out an exuberant cheer, and turned to face Dr. Martin's crew. "Better luck next time," she said with a grin.

"I was just going to say the same thing to you," one of them said, pointing to the water. *The Sea Wasp* had blocked the entrance to the resort's small harbor, and Dr. Martin was standing on the deck, tossing huge nets overboard.

Barnaby was swimming happily back to the lagoon, when he saw the huge fishnets spanning the length of the bay. He tried to rip them, but they were made of strong stuff. He threw his body against them, but he was bounced right back. Frustrated, he swam beside the mesh, searching for an opening. There was none. Finally, he stopped swimming and stared at his prison bars.

Sabrina and Gwen were standing at the end of the dock, watching angrily as the crew of *The Sea Wasp* threw huge nets into the bay. The nets were so big, Sabrina was sure that they would block the tiny waterway that led to the open sea. *How will Barnaby get back to the mermaid lagoon? There's no way he can get through those nets . . . My magic certainly picked a good time to fizzle out on me!*

Sabrina gazed long and hard at the white yacht in the harbor and turned to Gwen. "We've got to get out to that boat." Gwen nodded, and looked back toward the resort. The mob of tourists was leaving the resort and heading toward the dock.

"Quickly. I think the crowd is heading this way," said Gwen, pointing at the swelling group of excited people rushing down the resort's beachside pathway.

Suddenly, there was a splash in the water, and Spout's large snout burst out, his tail swishing playfully behind him. He squeaked and flopped onto his back, swimming happily below the dock.

"Spout. Perfect," said Sabrina, with a relieved smile. "My favorite taxi service." Spout nodded his head and flicked his tail in complete agreement.

"Meet me out there," said Sabrina to Gwen, pointing at *The Sea Wasp* far out in the bay. Sabrina dove into the water and disappeared under a large wave. She popped to the surface, and laughed as Spout tickled her face with his snout. He patiently waited for her to slide onto his back. When she had a firm grip around his neck, he squeaked once more, flapped his tail and swam toward the white yacht in the bay.

"Meet you out there?" said Gwen, watching Sabrina disappear over a wave, riding her dolphin like a horse over hill country. "How am I supposed to meet you there? You took the last dolphin . . ." Gwen looked at the water below and scowled. Then, she looked down at her hands and the scowl turned into a smile. "Oh, right. It's worth a shot. I am kind of on a roll."

She cleared her mind of everything—the horde of crazed tourists stampeding down the path, her fear of messing up the spell, and her concern for Barnaby. She gazed defiantly at *The Sea Wasp*, slowly clenched her fist, and disappeared from the dock.

She reappeared, moments later, staring at *The Sea Wasp*'s deck. "Yes!" she cried happily, raising her arms with a cheer. But then she looked down. She had missed the boat by a couple of feet and was suspended ten feet in the air above the water.

"Oh, fizzle," she said weakly, plummeting into an oncoming wave with a big splash.

Fin was in the open ocean behind *The Sea Wasp*, watching the crazy scene unfold before her. She shook her head, tossing her golden tendrils in the sea foam, and disappeared back underwater.

Spout and Sabrina had reached the back of the yacht. Sabrina leaned close to his face and whispered, "Spout, I'm going to need you to do me one more favor . . ." He nodded happily and flapped his tail against the passing waves.

Barnaby was sitting on the ocean floor, staring at the nets that blocked his way to freedom. He became angry. Very angry. He pushed back on his tail, pulling up seaweed and sand on the ocean floor, and then he sprung toward the net with his considerable strength. The net sagged under his assault, and then it sprung back and around him, and he panicked, fighting the net as if it were a sea monster. As he struggled, his tail burst through the net, and got stuck in the unforgiving fabric. He twirled desperately in the water, trying to untangle himself, but with each twist and turn of his body, he only furthered the net's hold on his tail. In desperation, he looked out toward the open ocean, and saw the beautiful face of his sister, Fin, swimming toward him.

She paused when she reached the net, and placed her hand alongside his. They stared into each other's eyes sadly. She swam down to his tail and began to gently unwind the torn pieces of the net.

* * *

Gwen was swimming around the side of the boat, searching for a way up. She spotted Sabrina gingerly climbing the rope ladder. She called out and waved, pushing through the water and grabbing onto the bottom rung.

Sabrina looked down at her, amused. "You swam?" she asked, trying not to smile. Gwen pulled herself up higher and said with a sniff, "I was afraid I wasn't getting enough exercise on this holiday."

Fin darted around Barnaby's tail, carefully unwinding pieces of the net, and trying to rip some with her delicate hands. Barnaby held the net and shook it, his frustration growing with each passing second. Fin reached up to reassure him, and gently touched his tail with her rainbow-colored fin. He looked down at her with large sad eyes, melting and liquid blue like the water around them.

Sabrina and Gwen jumped off the ladder and onto the boat's deck, unseen. Dr. Martin and his assistant were looking over the other side of the boat, trying to spot Barnaby. There was a large pile of nets near them, and a pulley device that they had used to lower some of the nets into the water. Some of the nets were attached to the side of the deck with huge clips. Sabrina motioned to Gwen and they ran to one of the clips and began to pull on it. It finally snapped off and a portion of the net sagged, useless in the water.

Fin had successfully freed Barnaby's tail, and when he noticed the weakness in the net, he pushed through it and swam into the side of freedom, back toward home.

Sabrina was just about to unhook another section when a large, suntanned hand clamped down upon hers. *Uh oh . . .*

She looked up and saw Dr. Martin's grim face scowling down at her. "Game is over, Sabrina. You're very clever, but no one makes a fool of me on my reef."

His assistant came running over. "Julian, I think we've got him." They rushed over to the side and began to pull in the net.

"This will give those rubes back at the resort something to write about," said Dr. Martin, giving the net another strong yank.

"No!" Sabrina cried, rushing over to him. "You can't do this."

They ignored her and continued pulling up the net, until its contents spilled onto the deck. Dr. Martin and his assistant stepped back, stunned. Long, flowing golden hair was tangled in the harsh mesh. Her beautiful face and sea-blue eyes flushed with fear. Her tail flipped in its prison of ropes, the tiny scales bursting with sunlight and dripping with kisses from the sea.

"Fin!" cried Sabrina, kneeling by the net and reaching for her hand, struggling to hold back tears of anger.

"Sabrina? What's happening?" said Fin, dazed and terrified behind the net. "Why are you doing this?" she whispered.

Barnaby and Spout surfaced with a rush of excitement. They were free! Barnaby flipped into the water, swam down and waved at schools of colorful fish passing by. He laughed and flew back up to the surface, about to do his favorite dive, a double back flip, when something on the deck of *The Sea Wasp* caught his eye. His eyes narrowed, and he said softly, "Fin?" He and Spout gazed sadly at the boat. Barnaby took a deep breath and dove back into the water.

"Over here!" he cried, bobbing in the water near the deck. He raised his arms and waved them wildly. "Over here!" he said, desperation once again filling his heart.

The Sea Wasp crew stared at his shape in the water, their eyes lighting up with excitement.

"Barnaby, go away!" Fin cried. "Get out of here!" She tried to rip the net from her body, but she knew she wasn't strong enough. She lay back down, tears cascading down her cheeks like a gentle waterfall.

"Let's see if we can get a net around that one, too," said Dr. Martin, rushing with his crew to the other side of the boat.

Suddenly, Spout popped out of a wave, playfully squeaking. "Sabrina," said Gwen, pointing to the water. "Look!"

"Spout. Did you find it?" asked Sabrina. Spout squeaked, dove below the surface and flicked something wet and colorful into the air. Sabrina reached out and caught the beautiful yellow fish, with a fake eye glowing and shimmering on its tail.

"Sabrina, it's your fish," said Gwen, rushing over. Sabrina smiled and gently stroked the blue oval down its side. *The blue-spot butterfly fish. If this doesn't remind Dr. Martin of what his priorities should be—that he's supposed to protect all of the creatures of the sea—then I don't know what will!*

Chapter 13

Dr. Martin spun around and stared at the fish in Sabrina's hand. He ran his hand through his hair and sighed softly. He stepped closer and admired the sleek fish, his eyes wide with wonder.

"*Chaetodon plebeius.* Incredible," he murmured, stroking the soft fins as if they were silky petals. "It's beautiful." He turned back to his crew and shouted, "Quick! Somebody get me a bucket. We don't want to hurt it. Sabrina, be careful."

Sabrina raised her eyebrows and gave him a long, hard stare. "Actually, I was thinking of having it stuffed and hung on my wall. Now I'll have something to show the crowd back at the resort, too."

Dr. Martin handed her a bucketful of seawater, and she placed the fish gently inside.

"Don't worry, your little analogy isn't lost on me.

But this isn't the same thing," he said, gesturing toward Fin lying in the tangled net on the bottom of the deck. "I'm trying to protect . . ."

"What?" Sabrina interrupted. "Your ego? Your reputation?"

Dr. Martin looked out at the open sea and watched Barnaby waving frantically in the waves. "Sabrina, no one cares more about this reef than I do."

Sabrina pointed angrily at Fin. "You think you care more than she does? They live here. This is their home. We're all just guests here, remember. Even you."

Dr. Martin's gaze never moved from the merman and the dolphin swimming side by side in the blue-green sea.

"You call it 'your reef.' But it's not. It's theirs," she said softly, her eyes following his back to the figures in the water. "If you do this," she continued, "you're no better than the guys stealing coral."

Dr. Martin said nothing, and paced along the side of the deck. He stopped and knelt beside Fin. After a few moments, he pulled out a long knife and cut the net that held her hostage. Dr. Martin looked deeply into Fin's glowing eyes and said simply, "I'm sorry."

Fin nodded her forgiveness and rolled back into the arms of the waiting sea. Barnaby was by her side in moments, untangling her from the mesh. She tossed the net aside and clasped Barnaby's hand. They swam side by side through the crystal clear water, on their way home.

Everyone on board *The Sea Wasp* watched the merman and the mermaid swim out toward the open sea. Their beautiful tails sparkled and glowed all the colors of the rainbow as they darted in and out of the frothy waves. Fin's long, blond tresses cascaded around them like a protective blanket, gently undulating in the blue-green sea.

They're on their way home, thought Sabrina happily. She was blown away by their gentle radiance, their kindness and their beauty. *Of all the amazing creatures I have met along the way—whether from this realm or the other one—nothing can beat hanging out with two of the coolest mer-siblings on Earth . . .*

Sabrina's aunts hit the deck with a loud thud. "Ouch," said Hilda, pulling herself up by a nearby railing. "Not bad," she said, taking in the view. They landed on a beautiful yacht, anchored in the bay. Fresh, white paint glowed in the afternoon sun, and the interior cabins were made of rosewood, with ornate plates hanging on the wall next to old watercolors of famous ships from long ago. Porcelain vases bursting with fresh cut flowers lined the deck around them, perfuming the air. Waves rocked the boat gently, and the breeze that blew through her blond hair was warm and sweet.

Zelda smiled and zapped them into bathing suits with soft towels and suntan lotion lying at their feet. "You know how I feel about too much sun," she said happily.

Two men walked onto the deck, wearing spotless white uniforms, carrying trays of iced tea and plates of fresh fruit, gooey chocolate-chip cookies, and cheese and crackers. One of the young men bowed in greeting, and winked appreciatively at Hilda. *Hmm,* thought Hilda. *Very hunky guys—with good taste, too, as Sabrina would say . . .*

Another man came out and led them to two reclining lounge chairs that faced the open ocean. The view was as simple and clear as it was breathtaking.

"Ladies, would you care for your massage now?" he asked respectfully. Zelda smiled at her sister and nodded happily.

The afternoon passed quite well. After they enjoyed their sumptuous snacks, they were massaged, manicured, petted, fed more gourmet delights, bathed in luxurious herbal wraps and left alone in the afternoon sun to doze dreamily.

"You know, Zelda," said Hilda, gazing over at her sister who was lazily flipping pages of *Physics for Witches,* "these delightful young men don't appear to have Australian accents."

"Hmm," said Zelda, turning another page.

"And, as you were so eager to point out when we were freezing our pointing fingers off at the North Pole, or standing on an ice cap, or a glacier in Alaska—wherever it was—there don't seem to be any furry koala bears chomping on eucalyptus leaves here either. And I don't see any dolphins shooting out of the sea to play with us. I certainly don't see a single palm tree, though I can kind of make out an old maple tree, and maybe a group of pine trees . . . But, definitely, no barracuda in the water, no coral reef out in the distance and not a single tropical, well, anything . . ."

Zelda's lips curled up into a tiny smile, but she said nothing.

Hilda stared at her and frowned. *What's she hiding?* she wondered. Then, she looked farther out in the bay, toward shore. "There's something familiar about this place," she said thoughtfully. Her eyes narrowed. Her sister was up to something. What was it? She could just make out the small white houses near the beach, and the fishing boats that dotted the water. She looked into the open sea and spotted a fishing boat anchored close by. A fisherman was hauling wooden crates out of the water.

"Look!" cried Hilda. "He just pulled a lobster trap from the sea! Zelda, you took us back to New England."

Zelda smiled and put down her book. "After our whirlwind tour of the world, it's nice to be home again, isn't it?"

Hilda nodded and smiled sweetly at her older sister.

Zelda smiled her big sister smile in return. "You know, Hilda, even though the Earth's jet stream kept blowing us off course, it really was a magical trip. We started our adventure seeing the lovely London skyline, and then, well, the golf course incident I could have done without, but then, an afternoon in Venice? Truly delightful. And how often do we get to experience the excitement of raiding pirates? Hear the boom of the cannons, and smell the black smoke rising into the air?"

"And," added Hilda happily, "we petted a seal and ran from a polar bear—"

"I think we used our free time well, don't you?" interrupted Zelda with a contented smile. "And, we deserve a little pampering after all of that adventure. There really is nothing like home . . ."

"I hope Sabrina feels the same way after her wonderful trip," said Hilda, lying back down on her lounge chair with a satisfied sigh.

No one spoke during the ride back to the dock. Dr. Martin steered the ship, a look of firm determination on his face. The others were thoughtful and reflective; they had all witnessed something magical in the deep waters near the bay, something they would never forget.

After they docked, Sabrina carried the bucket with the blue-spot butterfly fish and walked next to Dr. Martin up to the resort. A large crowd of curious guests and reporters was still gathered outside the lobby. They rushed out to meet them, a look of keen expectation on their faces. The manager pushed his way through the people and rushed to Dr. Martin's side.

"Finally, some answers. Dr. Martin, you clearly told me that you'd made a discovery of monumental proportions," said the manager, his face flushed in the afternoon sun.

"I didn't make it," said Dr. Martin softly. "Sabrina did."

Sabrina held out the bucket. "Look," she said, smiling broadly, "the blue-spot butterfly fish. No one has seen it for fifty years. Cool, huh?"

The manager's face fell. Clearly he didn't think it was cool at all. The crowd of onlookers started to disperse, losing interest in such a small prize.

"You got us out here for some four-inch fish?" said a reporter with thinly veiled contempt. "I thought you said they had a mermaid."

Sabrina laughed. "A mermaid? You must be from the tabloids."

The manager grabbed Dr. Martin and looked pleadingly into his eyes. "What did you do with it? Please. I have the Coast Guard on the way . . ."

Dr. Martin smiled grimly and shook off his hand. "Seems like overkill, but they can help me cordon off the area."

"What?" cried the manager. "You can't do that."

Dr. Martin pointed at the little yellow fish in the bucket. "Thanks to our little friend here, I can. The National Endangered Species Act requires that the entire eastern half of the island be reclassified as a preservation zone. Entry into the area is completely forbidden, except for scientific research."

The manager stared at the little fish, completely baffled. "But it's such a small fish . . ."

Salem pranced happily down the hallway toward Hillary's room, holding a long-stemmed red rose in his mouth. He stopped short when several porters, carrying two bulging suitcases, stepped out from her doorway.

"Hillary?" said Salem to the half-closed door. "Hillary, what's the matter? Why are you leaving? Is it something I said? My breath?"

From behind the door, Hillary said, "Salem, I'm sorry. I was hoping I wouldn't have to say good-bye like this."

"Apparently," said Salem dryly, "you weren't planning on saying good-bye at all."

She sighed wearily. "Salem, I . . . I haven't been honest with you." She opened the door, revealing a stunning woman. "I'm already a woman," she finished softly.

Salem dropped the rose on the lush carpet. *"Meee-ow-ow-ow . . ."* he cried appreciatively.

A warm smile lit up her face, and she scooped him up into her arms. "I should have told you. This trip was to celebrate the end of my sentence. It expired today. I don't have to be a cat anymore. I'm a witch again." She gently stroked his black fur.

Salem leaned against her and sighed dreamily.

"That's perfect. I can come live with you, and in another eighty-seven years I'll be a man, and . . ."

"Salem, this is good-bye. I'm really more of a dog person." She set him back down on the carpet, and prepared to walk down the hall.

"But you said you loved me," said Salem, his large yellow eyes glowing sadly against the darkness of his fur.

Hillary paused and looked down at him. "I know. I think I was caught up in the moment. My therapist says I have a real problem with that."

Salem whimpered as he watched her make her way down the hall, her high heels digging deeply into the rug with every step.

The lobby was quiet, with a few guests reclining on chairs, gazing out at the pool and the sun deck below. Jerome and Gwen were standing in the middle of the lobby, surrounded by his duffel bags, gazing dreamily into each other's eyes. The sun streamed in through the sun roof, bathing them in a gentle light. Jerome wrapped two strong arms around Gwen's much smaller frame. He pulled her in for a long, sweet, sandy kiss. Gently, he let her go, grabbed his bags and headed for the door. He turned back once more and waved, his smile warm and sincere.

"You okay?" asked Sabrina, placing her arm around her friend's shoulder.

"I'll be fine," said Gwen dreamily. "He said he'd

write me every day . . . or else it was something about soccer. I never could figure out that accent." They burst out laughing and walked out into the afternoon sun.

The next day, Sabrina and Gwen were heading out of their bungalow, walking down the path toward the resort's lobby. "Come on," said Sabrina, "Dr. Martin is going to have a press conference."

When they entered the lobby, the place was jam-packed. Rows of chairs had been set up facing a small podium. The manager was standing next to some reporters on one side of the crowded lobby. Cameras flashed as Dr. Martin walked in front of the group, holding some blown-up photographs.

He stood on top of the podium and cleared his throat. "Since we have you all here, I wanted to let you in on another little discovery that we made yesterday."

The manager jumped in quickly. "Thanks to the dedicated efforts of one of our most loyal guests, Mr. Saberhagen, who unfortunately couldn't be with us this afternoon, we have identified the ship that is contaminating the reef and harming the marine life."

Dr. Martin displayed the blown-up photograph. The bottom was a shot of Hillary's head, but rising behind it was a very clear view of a large ship.

"The photos have been forwarded to the authorities and arrests have been made," said Dr. Martin gravely.

Salem was seated in the front row on the lap of a very attractive woman, who clearly appeared to be a cat person. Salem winked happily at Sabrina and leaned against his new mistress. "Oh, you are just the cutest little thing," she whispered into his ear, gently stroking his back.

"Me-ow," he purred in agreement.

Dr. Martin steered the inflatable Zodiac far out into the bay. Sabrina and Gwen were sitting on the side of the boat in their diving gear, happily dangling their legs in the rolling waves. The boat came to a stop, and Sabrina leaned over the side. She poured the blue-spot butterfly fish back into the water. Silently, they watched it swim through the clear sea toward the coral reef.

"Are you sure you don't want to come?" asked Sabrina, turning around to face Dr. Martin.

He nodded. "I'm sure. I think you've already got two of the best guides on the reef."

Barnaby and Fin were swimming playfully farther out in the bay. They waved, waiting for their friends to join them.

The mermaid and merman showed them all of the secrets hidden in the Great Barrier Reef. They swam past swirling schools of surgeonfish, cod and angelfish, feeling their silky fins against their hands. They picked radiant underwater flowers, bursting with color, and pushed through seaweed forests to uncover the giant turtles, lazy and slow in the afternoon stillness.

They swam through coral lagoons, amazed at how calm and clear the water was and dove to the bottom to greet the plenitude of mussels and clams.

Fin took Sabrina's hand and led her down though the shallow, warm water to the oyster bed, hidden under sea anemones and lush, green seaweed. The outer surface of the oyster shells seemed rough and bulbous next to the soft sand that surrounded them. Fin grabbed an oyster and expertly cracked it open against a nearby rock. She pulled out a gleaming, shiny pearl, glowing white and creamy pink against the sun-kissed blue of the waves. She opened Sabrina's hand and gently placed it inside, smiling sweetly.

Sabrina clasped the soft pearl in her hand, her eyes bright with wonder. *This is a perfect gift from a mermaid,* she thought, stroking the soft, iridescent pearl.

They swam near the side of the reef, its browns, oranges and yellows rising majestically out of the high waves. Starfish by the thousands lined the side of the coral, and it seemed to Sabrina that they were waving hello with their many legs.

Barnaby led them down into an underwater cave, where schools of fish—orange, red, yellow and blue—swirled around them, their long fins floating behind them like colorful scarves. They swam through the darkness, dimly lit by the glowing algae that lived on the rocky walls, and surfaced farther out at sea.

The waves lifted the four friends high in the deep water and then gently placed them down again. A school of gray whales had joined them, and water poured out of their blow holes like gushing fountains. The enormous animals moved like graceful swans, pushing up out of the waves to breathe, and then diving below again, their huge mouths open wide, combing the open sea for plankton. Their whale song was loud and clear, playing like a symphony of friendship.

Sabrina and Gwen watched, transfixed, as Barnaby swam up to the whales. He seemed so small next to their tremendous size. He rested an arm on one of the whales and pressed his ear against its snout, listening to its song with delight.

Barnaby rolled onto his back and swam toward the girls, the scales on his tail shining like evening stars against the water.

Soon, a group of dolphins joined in the fun, playfully darting out of the water and nudging them with their soft snouts. They swam with the dolphins through the rising waves, laughing as Fin clasped her arms around Spout and twirled round and round in the water. With her hair streaming behind her and her tail flickering the colors of the rainbow, she was as graceful as a ballerina.

At the mermaid lagoon, they surfaced and held hands in a circle, Fin's luminous blond hair swirling and dancing around them like a good luck spell.

This is definitely the most awesome experience I've ever had, thought Sabrina, laughing into Barnaby's sea-blue eyes. *Better than anything I could conjure up in my wildest imagination . . .*

About the Author

Ellen Titlebaum lives in New York City in an apartment with a garden. She has always secretly believed that she has magical powers of her own (she's still perfecting her conjuring spell for making her rosebushes bloom), and she was delighted to explore her powers in *Sabrina Down Under.* She has written many books for younger children, including *I Love You, Winnie the Pooh!, Winnie the Pooh and the Family Tree,* and adaptations of *Alice in Wonderland* and *Beauty and the Beast.*

Put a little magic in your everyday life!

Magic Handbook

Patricia Barnes-Svarney

Sabrina has a Magic Handbook, full of spells and rules to help her learn to control her magic. Now you can have your own Magic Handbook, full of tricks and everyday experiments you can do to find the magic that's inside and all around you!

From Archway Paperbacks
Published by Pocket Books

2021-01

American S·I·S·T·E·R·S

Join different sets of sisters
as they embark on the varied,
sometimes dangerous,
always exciting journeys
that crossed America's landscape!

West Along the Wagon Road, 1852

◆∽

A Titanic Journey Across the Sea, 1912

◆∽

Voyage to a Free Land, 1630

◆∽

Adventure on the Wilderness Road, 1775

By Laurie Lawlor

A MINSTREL BOOK
Published by Pocket Books

2106

Boys. Clothes. Popularity. Whatever!

Based on the major motion picture from Paramount
A novel by H.B. Gilmour

Cher Negotiates New York
An American Betty in Paris
Achieving Personal Perfection
Cher's Guide to...Whatever

And Based on the Hit TV Series

Cher Goes Enviro-Mental
Baldwin From Another Planet
Too Hottie To Handle
Cher and Cher Alike
True Blue Hawaii
Romantically Correct
A Totally Cher Affair
Chronically Crushed
Babes in Boyland
Dude With a 'Tude
Cher's Frantically Romantic Assignment
Southern Fried Makeover
Bettypalooza

1202-12

No mission is ever impossible!

Join the

on all of their supercool missions
as they jet-set around the world
in search of truth and justice!

The secret is out! Read

LICENSE TO THRILL
LIVE AND LET SPY
NOBODY DOES IT BETTER
SPY GIRLS ARE FOREVER
DIAL "V" FOR VENGEANCE
IF LOOKS COULD KILL

Available from Archway Paperbacks

2037-02